The Pecos Kid Returns

A Western Duo

Other Five Star Titles
by Dan Cushman:

In Alaska with Shipwreck Kelly
Valley of a Thousand Smokes
Blood on the Saddle
The Pecos Kid

The Pecos Kid Returns

A Western Duo

DAN CUSHMAN

Five Star
Unity, Maine

Five Star Western Series.
Published in 2000 in conjunction with
Golden West Literary Agency

"Raiders of the Stage Trails" first appeared in *The Pecos Kid Western* (1/51). Copyright © 1950 by Popular Publications, Inc. Copyright © renewed 1978 by Dan Cushman.

"Tamers of the Deadfall Towns" first appeared in *The Pecos Kid Western* (3/51). Copyright © 1951 by Popular Publications, Inc. Copyright © renewed 1979 by Dan Cushman.

The text of this edition is unabridged.

Set in 11 pt. Plantin by Al Chase.

Printed in the United States on permanent paper.

Library of Congress Cataloging-in-Publication Data
Cushman, Dan.
    The Pecos Kid returns : a Western duo / Dan Cushman.
        p.   cm.
    ISBN 0-7862-2114-3 (hc : alk. paper)
    1. Western stories. I. Title.
PS3553.U738 P44 2000
813'.54—dc21   00-037177

Table of Contents

Raiders of the Stage Trails

Tamers of the Deadfall Towns

Editor's Note

In the literary history of Western fiction magazines, some of the most popular authors of Western stories have had magazines named after them. *Zane Grey's Western Magazine*, published by Dell Publishing Company, began publication with the November, 1946 issue and continued for eighty-two issues, concluding publication with the issue dated January, 1954. *Max Brand's Western Magazine* was launched by Popular Publications, Inc., with the issue dated December, 1949, and continued for thirty-three issues, concluding with the issue dated August, 1954. *Walt Coburn's Western Magazine* commenced publication from Popular Publications, Inc., with the issue dated November, 1949, and after sixteen issues ceased publication with the issue dated May, 1951. *Louis L'Amour's Western Magazine*, published by Dell Magazines, began with an undated issue published in March, 1994, and continued for twelve issues, concluding with the issue dated January, 1996. *The Pecos Kid Western*, initiated by Popular Publications, Inc., with the first issue dated July, 1950, was a little different. Like *The Masked Rider Western* or *The Rio Kid Western*, pulp magazines published by the competing Standard Magazines, *The Pecos Kid Western* featured a long short novel in every issue about the Pecos Kid, but unlike most of the Western hero pulp magazines all of these stories were written by a single author, Dan Cushman, who had created the character especially for *The Pecos Kid Western*. The year 1950 was not an auspicious time to be creating a new pulp magazine, since pulp magazines were being replaced on newsstands by paperback books, many of them being published by magazine publishers like Dell Publishing. Despite the hostile market in 1950, *The Pecos Kid Western* did continue publication for five issues, concluding with the issue dated June, 1951. The stories about the Pecos Kid that Dan Cushman wrote for this magazine have not otherwise been available since their first publication. THE PECOS KID (Five Star Westerns, 1999) contains the first two short novels Dan Cushman published about the adventures of this fascinating character of the Old West. The present volumes contains two more adventures.

Raiders of the Stage Trails

I

"Three Masked Men"

After a long wait, as darkness settled on the mountain road, there was a grate of coach wheels from the top of the pass, and the Pecos Kid stood up, extinguishing his cigarette. "I reckon," he said in his easy Texas drawl, "that you-all are about to become coach robbers. That is, provided you're not already."

He had two companions. One was a huge young man of twenty-five with placid features and hair the color of burlap sacking; the other was smaller, with jet in his hair, and a mobile, handsome face.

The big fellow said in a voice that was unexpectedly treble: "Gosh, Kid, I never had anything to do with coach robbin', and I can't say I got any hanker to rob one now. Robbin' coaches can be dangerous."

"Danger, poof!" said the dark one in a south-of-the-border accent. "Danger . . . eet is the wine of my life, the sweetheart of my soul. In all Chihuahua was there ever a more reckless *caballero* than Hernandez Pedro Gonzales y Fuente Jesús María Flanagan?"

"You're a hell of a long way from Chihuahua now." William Calhoun Warren, the Pecos Kid, yawned, stretched himself, and held up a hand for quiet. There was no longer any sound of the coach. It had swung inward against the mountain, taking the hairpin bend along the head of Bird Tail Gulch.

In a straight line the coach was no more than half a mile

11

away, but the road, winding along switchbacks, would travel four times that distance before reaching them. They still had a little wait.

Working slowly, as though he had unlimited time at his disposal, the Pecos Kid took off his Confederate cavalryman's hat, fitted a black neckerchief with eyeholes into the sweatband, and tried it on. He was a slim man of twenty-eight or thirty, six feet tall, with a frame that would have accommodated one hundred and eighty pounds, but a life of hard riding had taken off every last ounce of fat so he weighed a scant one hundred and sixty. He had a long, lean jaw. Bird track wrinkles lay in the corners of his mouth and eyes, but, when he smiled, the hardness dropped away, and there was something boyish and reckless about him.

He smiled now as he looked at Big Jim Swing who was trying to get a couple of slits in his bandanna adjusted to his eyes.

"Only way to disguise you would be to saw your legs off. Aren't five men in this Montana-Idaho gold country big as you."

Big Jim finally got it so he could see through the slits. He drew his six-shooter. It looked small in his massive hand. He was nervous, and whispered: "Damn it all."

Pecos said: "Get the sawed-off. In this country, road agents 'most always favor sawed-offs. You don't want the coach driver to think you're a Pike's Peaker, do you?"

Big Jim, still cursing under his breath, got the sawed-off shotgun as Pecos told him. It was an old-time, muzzle-loading percussion piece. He took the caps out and put them back again. He stood stiffly, listening while the coach wheels grated nearer. The leather-faced brake shoes could be heard, too, groaning against the tires as the coach dropped down steep grades from the crest of the pass.

Pecos said: "Now, listen . . . don't get trigger-itchy. Neither of you. I don't want any dead driver or shotgun guard. And I sure as hell don't want any dead passengers."

Jim muttered: "They'll think it's damn' funny if we don't rob the passengers."

"They'll be too scared to think. I know. I got robbed down in New Mexico one time. I was too scared to think."

"I'm too scared to think myself."

Hernandez turned from his place among dwarf junipers by the road, saying: "Scared? What sort of *gringo* talk is thees? Let me tell you of my uncle, General Ramón Telesforo Julio y Aldasoro de Santillo Fuente. He was *caballero de la libertad,* fighter for liberty in the revolution . . . each revolution when she came along. Now, for money to pay his brave men two *pesos* each month in wages, did my uncle . . . *el general* . . . attack the stagecoach of the enemy political party, those tyrants, the Democratic Liberal Republicans. Alone, weeth two guns did he stop thees coach, and on it, besides passengers, were one . . . two . . . three shotgun guards and one squad of horsemen from the government *caballería.* But was my uncle . . . *el general* . . . afraid? No, he was not. Let me tell you what. . . ."

Pecos said: "Gentlemen, you seem to be interested in forensics."

"Forensics? What is thees?"

"That, seh, is talk for the sake of it, and in this case too damned much. Butch, you better get that handkerchief down."

Hernandez got his mask down and crouched once again by the road, a six-shooter weighting each hand, his head up, listening as the sounds of the coach grew loud, seemed ready to burst into view, then faded again.

Pecos walked into the road, stepped over the fir tree that

had been felled as a block, and said over his shoulder: "You know your jobs. Just let 'em know you're there and let 'em see your guns. I'll do the talking."

Uphill forty or fifty feet the road curved from sight around an almost perpendicular shoulder of stone. Moving swiftly, Pecos disappeared into scrub timber and came in view a few seconds later on a level with the huge rock he had reached on hands and knees. There he waited, hunkered, his guns still holstered.

He seemed perfectly relaxed, although excitement brightened his eyes. Through his teeth, very softly, he whistled a tune.

The coach was close now. Its clatter and grate of movement seemed to be almost atop him. He tensed forward a trifle, peering up the road, over the crest of the little promontory. The seconds seemed to drag along, then suddenly it was there, rolling through the fir trees.

It was a big coach, a Concord, pulled by six horses. Two men rode on the high seat. He could look down on their hats, on the sides of their faces, on their shoulders as they weaved and jounced, leaning as the coach maneuvered the close turn.

One of them, the guard, a heavy, black-whiskered man with a shotgun between his knees, moved to spit tobacco juice over the side. Then, peering away and downward through the trees, he said: "Thar it is! That's Butte. You can always get a glimpse of its lights from hyar. Dammit, I wish I was in Butte right now. I could do with a snort of something."

The driver, a tall, lean man with drooping mustaches, made some grunting answer through the effort of handling his team.

Pecos rose slightly, rocked forward. He was poised. Then, at the planned instant, just as the lead team got its first glimpse of the obstruction, he sprang, alighting on top of the

14

coach. Its weaving momentum for a second almost propelled him over the side. He went to his knees, grabbed the rail. Then, getting his balance, he drew both guns.

Amid excitement of the veering lead team with swing horses and wheelers overrunning them, the shotgun guard took a moment to realize that someone was behind him. He started to turn, but he froze at feeling the gun muzzle on his spine.

"Sure," Pecos said. "Live a while. You don't want to die for that other man's money."

The driver had his hands full, fighting the teams. He knew he'd get no help, and that there were other masked men below.

"All right. I'm peaceful."

"That's good, seh."

All six horses were stopped, the leaders among green twigs of the felled fir tree, the swing team and the wheelers at cross angles with the heavy coach almost overrunning them. Big Jim was on the hill side with his shotgun raised. Hernandez with a Colt in each hand stood to cover the passengers.

"Keep your hands up!" Hernandez cried in a voice with all the Spanish softness gone from it. "Hands up and stay inside or you will end up dead!"

A moment before, all the passengers had been shouting at once. They quieted suddenly, all except for a woman who had started to sob and an old man who kept beating his cane and shouting questions in a querulous voice.

"Damned dirty road agents," the driver was saying as, with reins between all his fingers, he controlled each of his horses with the right twist at just the right moment. "Now you tooken to robbing the *incoming* coaches! How much of the heavy color do you think you'll take off an *incoming* coach? They running sluice boxes in Kansas these days?"

15

"You take care o' your horses," Pecos said. He was up now, standing. "You!" he said to the guard. "Drop that shotgun over the side."

"Sure."

The guard very carefully lifted the gun, holding it by its fore end, and slid it stock first over the side. A nail had been driven there, and with a slight turn he caught it inside the trigger guard. At that instant the gun was aimed over his right shoulder at the position he sensed Pecos to be. With a tiny flinch of his wrist he tripped the trigger, and the gun exploded, driving flame and buckshot into the night. It scorched the side of Pecos's face, but he'd recognized the maneuver and shifted out of the way.

The horses were lunging again, dragging the snubbed coach. The guard, moving with the recoil of his gun, tried to go over the edge. Pecos swung his right-hand Colt. It struck the guard in the muscle where his neck and shoulder joined. It stiffened him. It left him in pain, twisting on his back, looking upward into the twin barrels of Pecos's .45s.

"You're lucky to be alive," Pecos said.

"Don't shoot!"

"I won't. You were just doing your job. But don't try pushing your luck any further."

The guard shook his head.

"Unstrap your pistols."

Still lying on his back, he did so. Then he sat up and weaved his head around, getting the pain out of his neck.

"Now the money box."

The guard leaned forward, reached down, got a two-hand hold on the heavy box. It was all he could do to lift it. He grunted, heaved upward, and let it fall overboard with a *clank*.

Pecos said: "Now let's have a look in the boot."

"There's nothing in that damn' plunder box. Just baggage...."

"Dump it out."

The guard obeyed, sliding over the stern boots first. The woman was still sobbing, and a man, speaking in a low voice, was trying to reassure her.

Hernandez, suspicious of someone, called out: "You, tall man! Keep your hands up or you will have your head blown off even with your shoulders."

"Nice fellows," said the driver, speaking over his shoulder to Pecos.

"We get along."

"This is the fifth time I been robbed this month. Got a guard kilt beside me t'other side o' Pipestone. You pull *that* piece o' business?"

"I might have."

"Might not have, too. I been robbed so damn' many times I know every road agent in the gold country by the smell of his sweat. Whar you hail from, down in I-dee-ho?"

"I been lots of places."

There was no second express box in the boot. Pecos gestured with one gun toward the heap of luggage. "Put it back, all of it."

"No, it *weren't* you!" The driver sounded almost friendly. "Last bunch o' varmints burned the baggage out of pure cussedness. Say, you ain't got a cigar on you? I could...."

"Take care of your horses."

"I'm caring for 'em."

Pecos leaped to the ground, told the guard to get back on top, and backed away up the rise of the mountain, saying: "You, inside! Get down and move the tree. But be careful. We'll riddle the first man that makes a false move."

Nine men piled down from the coach. It took them the

better part of a minute to drag the tree aside far enough so the driver, maneuvering along the edge of the road, could get the coach past. Then, waiting barely long enough for the last two of them to get back through the doors, he snapped his long lash and put the team in a dangerous, downhill gallop with the coach careening after.

Standing shoulder to shoulder beside the strongbox, Pecos and Hernandez watched it out of sight. Big Jim came up, stripped off his mask, and said: "Whew! I'd never make a coach robber. Don't ever ask me to do it again. Live a hundred years, I'd *never* be a coach robber."

II

"Hot Money"

It took six bullets from Pecos's guns to break inside the strongbox. Pawing its contents while Hernandez held sputtering sulphur matches, he found a carton of two dozen gold watches addressed to Levine and Solomon in Butte; a sack of money weighing thirty or forty pounds, filled with quarters, halves, and dollars; there were some bank folders, one containing cashier's checks against Jay Cooke & Co., New York, made out to the Regal Silver Mines; some vouchers from the Union Trust of Denver City; and there were several bundles of mint-new banknotes in ten-dollar denominations.

Pecos riffled the banknotes, saying: "Why, I believe we have a talent for this business."

Hernandez grabbed for some of the money and was shouldered out of the way.

"¡Señor! Let me get my hands on them. So much moneys. What could I do with thees?"

"You couldn't pay one tenth of your honest debts. Keep your hands off it."

"But only the feel of it, Keed. My hands they have been so long without the feel of green money."

"No."

"You theenk, perhaps, I would go south weeth some of these greenbacks . . . as the *gringo* says?"

"Yes, that's just what I think."

"Well, perhaps, but only feefty or a hundred dollars.

19

Surely of all these moneys, so beautiful, so green like the grass of springtime. . . ."

"Keep your dirty claws out of it."

The Pecos Kid gathered everything inside a couple of saddlebags that he tied on his horse, a rangy buckskin. Then, leading the way, he set out at a swift pace along the stage road, across a creek ford, and down a gulch that in time broadened to a sage-dotted valley.

Nearly an hour passed, and the moon was rising. The stage was still ahead of them, rolling across the bottoms, toward Butte City whose lights could be seen scattered uphill from Silver Bow Creek.

Big Jim said: "We better get the hell off this road."

"Why?" asked Pecos.

"Why! Damn it, because I don't want any rope around my neck."

The Kid laughed and kept riding. There were hard-rock mines on both sides now, their dumps making long, half-cone scars down the mountainsides. Placer diggings were deep cuts with hummocky fields of white gravel where the sluice tails were heaped.

Although the camp was scarcely more than ten years old, most of the placer mines had already been worked out and abandoned, although some big, low-grade diggings were still being operated full blast, with torches burning, and steady tons of gravel being wheelbarrowed to the headgates by lines of Chinese.

After another half hour of quiet, as the coach disappeared from sight and they followed it to the outskirt shanties of the town, Big Jim Swing reined in and cried: "We ain't going to ride straight in there. Even you wouldn't be idiot enough to do that."

Pecos said: "Why, no, I sure wouldn't. We're going in the back way."

"Where to?"

"Why, seh, where'd you think? To the Butte City offices of the Three Forks Freight and Coach Company."

"Listen . . . I tagged with you through range war and squaw cookin'. But this is too much. Drive up there and somebody'll recognize us. Masks be damned, somebody off'n that coach will *know*. They'll find that money, and we'll stretch rope."

"All right, Jim." He sounded a little tired, his temper drawn thin. "If you want to shuck out on this, why there's the whole Territory of Montana open to you."

"And what'll you do?"

"I told you. I'm paying a visit to McCabe of the Three Forks Line."

"Oh, the hell with it." Jim resigned himself. "If you want to get hung, I'll get hung with you. I'm no coward."

Hernandez, who for miles had seemed on the verge of sleep, jolting along with his head back and eyes closed, awoke to say: "Of course, you're no coward, Jeem. It is only that you are afflicted weeth brains which makes you out of place in thees company."

They rode among shacks and dugouts, through the crazy-crooked buildings of Chinatown, around the mountainous dumps of the Anaconda Mine, finally to stop against a high pole corral.

"This is it," Pecos said.

He dismounted, taking the saddlebags. Below, on the next terrace of the slope, stood a long, frame storehouse and, next to it, the stage office.

The stage itself was still out front, and there was a press of men around it. Pianos and fiddles made a discordant jangle from saloons and shebangs, and mixed with this they could hear voices, upraised, excited. They couldn't understand anything that was said.

21

They followed successive flights of rude stairs down the rock pitches of the hillside, Pecos still in the lead with the saddlebags, Hernandez next, whistling "Celito Lindo" through his teeth, and Big Jim, coming up in the rear with one hand clamped on the butt of a six-shooter.

They passed beneath a pole awning and looked inside the lamplit rear room of the stage station. It seemed to be a combination office and living quarters.

"Nobody home," said Pecos with satisfaction.

"Where is the guts, Keed? Why not the front door, like the gentleman, and not the back way like some sneaking *peon?*"

"Butch, we got a job to do. Risk for the hell of it doesn't appeal to me. I left all that kid stuff along the back trail. I left it a hell of a long way along the back trail. Come to think of it, I had my bellyful of risk at Vicksburg."

He went inside, dropped the bags with a heavy jingle of the silver money, and said: "Close the door and blanket that window. I wouldn't want it found out we visited McCabe."

They waited. After eight or ten minutes there was a whisper of footsteps, and Pecos blew out the lamp. It still wasn't quite dark. A lamp burned in the storeroom next to them, some of its glow entering through the open door. The feet had stopped.

Pecos moved to the door and saw a young Chinaman in soft slippers, loose cotton shirt, and trousers.

"We're waitin' for Pat McCabe. Old friends of his. Tell him to come."

"Ho, no. Missy McCabe ve'y busy. He don't see anybody. Stagecoach robbed. Lose two, three, four thousan' dolla. Missy. . . ."

"Sure. Tell him we got a line on the thieves. Tell him to come by himself."

"Ho, ve'y good!"

He left, running. In fifteen or twenty seconds a small man of middle years strode up to the door where he stopped, trying to make them out in the semi-darkness. With the light behind him, they could see he was rusty-complexioned, his hair just turning gray. His face had become pinched, but it still retained a hint of the Irish good temper of his youth. A Smith and Wesson .44 was strapped around his waist, and his right hand had come to rest on the butt.

He cried: "Why are you sittin' there in the dark?"

Pecos said: "We got our reasons. You're Mister McCabe, seh?"

"Yes, I'm McCabe."

"Then we have something to say to you." He saw that a large-shouldered young man and a blonde girl had followed him from the front of the building. He added: "It's *private*."

McCabe didn't move. He looked from one to the other, and said: "I don't know you. What could you have in private for me?"

"Are you interested, seh, in the identity of the men who just robbed your incoming coach?"

McCabe stiffened. Without another word he hooked the door and closed it, leaving the room quite dark.

"Dad!" the girl outside cried.

"Go along with you!" Then to Pecos: "*What* do you know about the robbery?"

Pecos lighted the lamp, adjusted the wick. "Why, we know nearly everything." He slid back his hat, revealing his front thatch of unruly brick-red hair. "We know how it was performed, we know where the money is, and we know the identity of the robbers."

McCabe barked: "How could you know so much?"

"Because, seh, the robbers happen to be *us*."

23

It took McCabe a moment to recover. "I'm in no mood to banter!"

"Me, neither." The Pecos Kid, with a grunting effort, lifted the saddlebags and dropped them on the table. He unfastened the straps. "I like a good wholesome joke as well as the next man, seh, but three thousand in greenbacks is no joking matter."

He dumped first one, and then the other saddlebag, and with a sweep of his hands spread their contents beneath the lamp for McCabe's scrutiny.

"It's all there, seh. Bank papers, cashier's checks, vouchers, watches, currency, silver money. I hope you'll excuse me for going about this in my own way. We had a communication on that score, if you will remember."

Suddenly McCabe laughed. He sat down, struck his forehead with the heel of his hand, and laughed again. "Well, I'll be damned! So that's who you are! So you're the Pecos Kid."

After shaking hands with Jim Swing and Hernandez, Pat McCabe, president of the Three Forks Freight and Coach Company, said: "If you don't mind, I'll call my daughter and the young man. He's my quarter partner, Captain John Coleman. I'm sure. . . ."

"Like I said, it has to be private, between us."

"But, man, look here! What if something happened to me and it was learned you robbed the coach? Why, it could lead. . . ."

"It could lead to hanging. I'll take that chance, seh. In a business like this, there's always a chance involved. I'd rather take *that* chance . . . of swinging for robbery . . . than the chance that your daughter or this Captain Coleman might talk when they should be listening. It's private, seh. Between *us*. Nobody else . . . *just us*."

"Oh, very well," McCabe said, and started to gather up the money.

"Leave it there," said Pecos.

He jerked erect. "What do you mean?"

"I mean we're keeping it. Why'd you think we went to all the bother o' robbing that coach when we could have been here in Butte, having a time for ourselves? Not for the good mountain air. I've had too much mountain air in my time and not near enough corn likker. No, McCabe. We did that to make road agents of ourselves. You go up and shout it from atop the Anaconda dump if you like, that Pecos, Hernandez Flanagan, and Big Jim Swing robbed your coach. I figure on using that bank paper to get on the right side of the wrong element in this camp. That's the only way we'll get to the bottom of who's been road agentin' your stage line into bankruptcy."

McCabe, flushing, cried: "Damn it, you have no need of the currency! You don't need to rid yourself of *that* through underground channels."

Pecos took a deep breath, and for a moment he was bitter-eyed. "Mister McCabe, you're welcome to *all* of it. I understand there's big things doing yonder, over the pass of Cœur d'Alene. We'll ride there. No hard feelings . . . shake hands and forget it. But if we stay and bust this road agent gang for you, it'll be done our way."

Once again McCabe drove the heel of his hand against his forehead, but this time he didn't laugh. "All right. I'm about at the end of my rope. You take it. I'll have to make it good some way, but you take it. Do it your own way."

III

"The Honky-Tonk Kid"

Plank walks went step-like down Butte's sidehill street from one noisy saloon to the next. After a quarter mile of them, the Pecos Kid stopped in front of a big, ramshackle building that bore a sign reading **The National**.

"Here it is," he said.

Big Jim stood tall, trying to see through the smoky windows. "What's he look like, this Ed Roe?"

"Why, I guess he's a real eyeful. Silk shirt and a velvet vest, diamond ring and a walking cane."

"Damn it, I don't like walkin' in there. I feel trapped inside. I don't mind risking my neck under the sky, but once I get closed in by four high walls and a roof. . . ."

"Then, *señor*, we will take eet apart," said Hernandez, showing his excellent teeth. "Like that crook joint in Maverly."

"We're not taking *this* joint apart," Pecos said, and went through the swinging doors.

The National had a bad reputation, but one would never guess that from first appearances. This was no plank and tincup affair. Its ornate back-bar must have been a tandem job for two freight wagons, and how it had been brought over the hump from Salt Lake was a marvel.

The big front room was all saloon. Gambling games lay beyond an ornate colonnade. Still farther away, out of sight, was a dance hall or theater, and the sound of fiddles and a piano in polka time came through the babble of voices.

Pecos said: "You wait. Have a couple of drinks." He looked at Hernandez. "Get that? . . . a *couple*. And stay away from the women. Get in any trouble tonight and I'm not pulling you out of it. You can go out feet first and the hell with you."

"And the hell weeth you, *señor*."

Pecos walked through the colonnade, quickly scanned the crowded gambling room. There was an archway entrance to the variety theater, and a door leading to some back rooms. Experience with a hundred places like The National told him he'd find the office there.

An ugly, heavy-jawed man jumped off the look-out stool by a faro game and grabbed Pecos's arm as he was about to go in. "Hold on. You can't go in there."

"Where's Roe?"

"I don't know."

"Call him."

"Say, listen, you're not giving *me* any orders. If you. . . ."

"I said . . . call him."

Something in Pecos's voice made him change his mind. He grumbled—"Well, wait here."—and started down a short length of hall. He realized Pecos was following and started around, but froze as Pecos rammed a forefinger in his back.

"Keep going."

"Yeah," he whispered. He rapped at a door. "It's me. Monk."

A nasal voice answered: "All right, come on in."

Ed Roe was a soft-looking man of thirty-five. He sat with his polished boots on the edge of a desk. He was probing at his teeth with a gold toothpick. He stopped and snapped his jaw shut when he saw Pecos. A couple of men who'd been talking to him turned to look.

27

Monk, with his hands half raised, said: "I couldn't help it, boss. He's got a gun in my back."

Everyone else could see it was just the Kid's forefinger, and they laughed.

"You damn' fool," Ed Roe said. Then to Pecos: "Well, who are you and what do you want?"

"Private matter." He looked at the others. "That's what I said . . . private matter. You want that dealt over? Get out!"

"You got your guts," Roe said, getting his boots down.

"Why, yes, seh." He watched the men go. When the door was closed, he took a money folder from his pocket and tossed it on the desk. "Look through that paper and see what it's worth."

Roe fingered the checks and vouchers. Suddenly he realized where they'd come from. "What the hell? Did you . . . ?"

"Sure. I got them off the coach."

"And had the guts to ride in here . . . ?"

"I'm a heller for sure," Pecos said flatly. "How much?" Roe started to object, but Pecos again cut him off. "Let's not play around. I know you take care of these things. You can have 'em passed in Helena and Benton at face value. Every road agent between here and The Hole knows that. I figure I ought to get at least sixty percent of face value."

Pecos sat tilted on the hind legs of his chair, watching through cigarette smoke, as Roe spent several minutes examining the papers. He noticed Roe's fingers trembled a little. Roe wasn't the kingpin of the road agent gang. He didn't have the force; he didn't have the cold nerve.

"It'll take some time," Roe said. "Will you stick around?"

"Don't worry. As long as you got those gold vouchers, I'll be around."

The Pecos Kid sat at a table near the wall of the jam-packed little theater and watched a middle-aged man and woman do an obscene song and dance on stage. It was a tough place in a tough town. It was filled with miners off the hill, with teamsters, with gunmen, with women and the men who lived off them.

He kept wiping sweat off his forehead. The air had all been used before. It was heavy with tobacco smoke and perfume.

The song ended, and for a long time the crowd stamped and roared its approval.

A girl in a thin silk dress sat down so close beside him he could feel the press of her shoulder. She said: "You lonesome, cowboy?"

She was about twenty-three. Her face was caked over with powder, and under it she looked tired.

"Where you from?" he asked.

"San Francisco."

"How'd you end up in a dive like this?"

"Say, what are you, anyhow? . . . one of them go thou and sin no more psalm-singers?"

"Forget it. Order a drink."

She called for wine. The waiter took Pecos's dollar and gave the girl a brass percentage check. Pecos drew one of the new ten-dollar bills from his pocket, folded it, and tucked it inside the bodice of her dress.

While she was still showing surprise and delight with the money, he took a casual shot in the dark. "Fellow always comes to visit Ed Roe after dark. Comes in the back way. What's his name?"

The delight left her face. She was scared. She got to her feet. "How would I know?"

"Who do the girls say it is?"

"You're barkin' up the wrong tree." She was about to leave. She stopped. "Listen . . . there was a fellow here about six nights ago, asking the same question. Know what happened to him? They found him shot cold, back by the Anaconda dump."

"Then I'll just keep away from the Anaconda dump."

"You better stay away from *here*. You seem to be a nice kid."

He watched her move away through the crowd. Nice kid! With the Civil War and two thousand miles of the frontier behind him, these girls from the houses still liked to call him a kid. He couldn't understand it. She was just a kid herself.

He waited. New acts kept appearing on stage. The heat and closeness of the place suddenly seemed unbearable. He stood up to leave. It was then he saw Monk, elbowing through the crowd, looking for him.

"Boss wants you," Monk said.

Ed Roe was alone in the office, boots on the desk, a long panatela cigar in his teeth. He was riffling the checks and vouchers like a deck of cards. He motioned toward a chair with his bloodless fingers and said: "Five hundred for the lot."

"For twelve thousand paper? That's less than five percent."

Roe shrugged. "Then pass them yourself."

"And end up with one of those vigilante hackamores around my neck?"

Roe took the panatela away from his teeth and dislodged the ash with his little finger. "You see? You go out there and do the butchering while somebody else gets the sirloin. Now if you worked with us, on the inside. . . ." He spread his fingers.

It was the invitation Pecos had planned for. He hid his swelling elation behind a downward twist of his lips and sat scratching a day's growth of whiskers along his jaw. He said: "Now, you got a thought there. You got a good thought. Personally I'd line up with the devil and the cohorts of hell if it'd put a little heavy color in my poke. I'm not alone, though. Got a couple of pals. Always deal 'em in. What sort of a deal do you suppose the boss of the Lodgepole Gang would give us?"

He didn't deny it was the Lodgepole Gang. "For the Pecos Kid, Big Jim Swing, and Hernandez Flanagan, it might be pretty good."

He was smug about having their names, and it jolted Pecos a little, but he didn't let anything show on his lean, weather-branded face. He said: "By the way, I'd like to know who I'm working for. Just who's the big boss of Lodgepole?"

"An old friend of yours. Sorry, no more information. I'll see if I can arrange a meeting for tomorrow night."

IV

"A Man Called Cole"

An old friend of his! Pecos lay in his room above The National and thought of a hundred men off the long back trail, and then slept.

He awoke with the clang and creak of freight outfits coming from the street below. He stood by the open window, stretched, and scratched. It had been his first night in a real bed since leaving Maverly, down in Wyoming Territory. A breeze, tainted by sulphide from a silver smelter, blew in, feeling good and cool on his naked skin.

He looked just in time to see Big Jim and Hernandez disappear inside of a Chinese café on another street. When he got there, they were half through a breakfast of salt pork and Mormon eggs.

Pecos sat on a stool beside the Spanish Irishman and said: "Looks like you got through the night in pretty fair shape."

"And what could I be but in good shape, broke and bankrupt in thees mining camp with the poorest tobacco-juice whisky costing four beets for one drink? *Señor,* do you know where I slept?"

Pecos yawned and said: "Had a featherbed myself."

"A featherbed . . . while the friends of your heart who have lived through range war and squaw-cooking by your side must be content to sleep with the horses in a feed stable?"

"Did you sleep in front of the horses or behind the horses?"

"In front of the horses, you cheap *gringo* saddle tramp, and now pay for the breakfast. We are without funds, and these Utah eggs cost at the rate of seex beets apiece." Hernandez was mollified by the sight of money. He ordered more eggs and said: "Did you speak with the leading light of those road agents?"

"Not yet. Chance of doing it tonight."

It rained hard, sending brownish torrents down the Butte gutters during the early evening, but some of the stars were out at ten o'clock when Ed Roe took them to the corral back of The National. Two men were waiting. Both were tall, thin, and in their middle twenties.

Roe introduced a rusty-complexioned one as Chevalier, the slightly smaller, darker one as Orofino Johnny.

"Your horses up at the Silver City Stable?" Chevalier asked. "Then we'll drift and wait for you at Pipestone." He winked and added: "I hear Ben Fillmore and McCabe are joining forces to import some gunmen on account of the road agentin' that's been goin' on. Five riders all in a bunch might make 'em suspicious."

Ben Fillmore, a frontier tycoon, was McCabe's bitter competitor for the coach and wagon freight business between Fort Benton and Butte City. There was little enough chance of them ever getting together on anything.

As they rode from town, Hernandez said: "Fillmore and McCabe's gunman talent. That's *us*, Keed."

"Fillmore doesn't even know we're here."

"McCabe knows. And why did the road agent mention it?"

"Oh, hell, nobody suspects us. The day we're suspected we'll be dead."

Hernandez grinned with a flash of teeth against dark skin.

"Now *thees* relieves my mind."

Hernandez took the slicker off his guitar and sang as they rode through the long ridges of placer tailings, and outward across the flats. His voice was untrained, but it had a flexible, lyric quality that was good to listen to. Pecos scarcely noticed the passage of time as one after another Hernandez sang the border songs. It had clouded over, and rain commenced falling again. Hernandez wrapped the guitar in the slicker, not caring if the rain soaked him.

"Pipestone yonder," Pecos said.

The road had started to climb into the mountains. Cut through white slide rock and evergreens, it looked like a strip of snow. They rode past one turn, and another.

"Hi-up!" a voice said.

Hoofs made a rattle at the side of the road. Chevalier and Johnny came into sight. There were slight movements from Pecos and Hernandez as they reholstered their guns.

"This way," Chevalier said, and put his horse up a steep climb from the wagon road.

They followed a winding game trail through slab rock and deadfalls. Rain still fell, but it made scarcely a whisper in the deep forest. The trail improved and followed a high contour around the mountain into a steep-sided gulch. They crossed a minor divide. It had stopped raining, with now the stars and then the moon coming out. They crossed a turbulent little creek. All around were mountains without prominent landmarks. There was another ridge, and beyond it a sparsely timbered valley.

Chevalier reined in, cupped his hands, called: "Shorty!"

A voice answered: "Who is it? Chev?"

"Yeah. Got three recruits."

A man limped into sight with a Henry rifle slung in the crook of his arm. "Three more? Hope they don't play poker like the last ones. That tinhorn you brought in here from I-dee-ho cleaned me."

Chevalier, riding closer, saw how heavy-lidded the man's eyes were and asked: "Wake you up?"

"Like hell! Cole would shoot my head off if he caught me sleeping on this job."

"He in camp?"

"Got in about sundown. He's still awake, too. Leastwise there's a light in the square house on top of the hill."

"Stay up all night?"

Shorty turned his back, but Pecos heard him growl under his breath: "Had a visitor."

"That *special* visitor?"

"Same one."

Chevalier whistled, laughed under his breath, and rode on, leading them across half a mile of meadow to some corrals of newly cut aspen poles. On a slight elevation, well removed from the nearest timber or natural protection that could be used for attack, stood a couple of log buildings. One was a long, shed-roofed bunkhouse, the other, with lighted parchment windows, was square, as Shorty had described it.

Chevalier, going to the door, found it empty.

A man was waiting nearby, concealed by shadow. "Go inside," he said. "One at a time."

His voice jolted Pecos. It was familiar, but momentarily he couldn't place it. His mind traveled far back, across trails and roundup camps and boom towns. Then, recalling Shorty's reference to Cole, he knew who it was. Cole Addis. Tall, easy talking, deadly Cole Addis. His *old friend,* as Ed Roe had called him. They'd covered lots of miles, he and Cole Addis, since they opposed one another in the bloody Clayton cattle war.

Chevalier went inside, and Pecos followed. He knew Cole

Addis had a gun ready. Briefly, with the light behind him, he was a perfect target. It gave him an itch between the shoulders, a buzz of excitement in his ears. Then he was hidden by the walls and still alive. He took a breath. It seemed stifling. He swept off his hat and wiped perspiration on his rain-damp shirt sleeve.

The others came in then with Cole Addis following. He stood in the door, fairly filling it, hands on his hips. They were careless hands, but habit had placed them just over the twin butts of his .45s. There wasn't a pound of fat on him anywhere. He was angular, big, erect, with good shoulders, handsome, with the side-of-the-mouth smile that came from habitually keeping his lips scissored on a cigarette. His eyes, very pale blue, alone detracted from his appearance. He was dressed in the best.

"Well, Pecos," he said, "so here we are together again. Who'd ever have thought it? Us meeting in a robber's roost. We both came a long way, but I guess you came the furthest. How'd it ever happen . . . *you* getting your fingers in a thing like coach robbery?"

"A man gets tired of being broke."

"Sure." Cole walked over and clapped him on the elbow with one hand while shaking hands with the other. He winked and grinned. "Well, you put up one hell of a fight on the side of the poor and needy down at Mescalero, I'll say that for you. By the way, did you keep tab on those nesters you helped in gobbling up that Rocking R range? Hear another crop of nesters showed up and started to squeeze *them*. I suppose they said . . . 'Come thou and take, for there's aplenty.' "

"Don't rub it in, Cole."

He laughed, said—"All right."—and shook hands with Hernandez and Big Jim.

It would be easy to like Cole, Pecos was thinking. Easy

until you met his eyes. Somehow those pale, deadly eyes changed everything.

Big Jim said in his unexpectedly high-pitched voice: "Well, what about those nesters? What *did* they do?"

Cole said: "What do you suppose? Took to shooting. In the back. Sure, those cold-meat notches. That's something the Rocking R never did. They went out and hired some guns, but they never got 'em in the back."

Pecos spoke with a knife-edge tone creeping in: "Don't try to rub it in."

"All right. Water over the falls." Addis sat down on the plank bench, crossed his legs, brushed a bit of pine needle off his cross-weave pants. The ends of his heavily weighted holsters, resting on the bench, made the butts of his Colts tilt outward. Speaking to Big Jim, he said: "Pecos and me were on opposite sides all through the Clayton war. We didn't start out top hands in that fracas, but we ended that-a-way. They killed Boze McClure, and we got Tall Charley Clayton. After that, Pecos and me had the tinhorns in Mescalero laying money which would walk and which would be carried when we run head-on, but the Army showed up, and it never happened."

He stood, and leaned over to light his burned-out cigarette from the grease lamp. The flame, shining close, took all the handsomeness from his face, making it big-boned, deeply cleft, and coppery. "And now we're partners. All bets are off. Nobody'll ever know."

As Addis stood up, Pecos caught the faint hint of perfume. Addis wasn't the type who used the stuff. Perhaps he'd carried it out from some place like The National, only this wasn't the rank stuff you'd find in a house like that. It was New Orleans; it was French.

Cole was watching him, his pale eyes intent. "Well, Pecos,

what do you think of our spread?"

"If I was a vigilante captain with thirty men at my back, I'd come down on you tonight and wipe you out."

"The same old Pecos! Listen, if you were a vigilante captain headed here, you'd have a bullet through your heart before you got out of Butte. We're big, Pecos. We're big and getting bigger. That's why we need a man like you. Man with officer's training. Man good enough to be major under Beauregard."

"Johnston."

"All right, then, Johnston. What's less important than the name of a defeated general?"

It always angered William Calhoun Warren—the Pecos Kid—when anyone made light of the Confederacy. His eyes hardened as he said: "Maybe a defeated road agent. They don't even get time to take their boots off."

Addis said: "You should know." He threw his cigarette away after taking only two puffs off it. "It's hot in here. Let's walk somewhere. Couple of things I'd like to take up with you."

It was sunup with a rough-looking gunman crew straggling out for grub pile when Pecos and his two companions found some unused bunks and spread their blankets.

When they were alone in the long, dim room, Big Jim leaned out of his bunk and said: "What'd Cole Addis have to say?"

"Matter of business. I'm in for a double share, with you and Butch good for one apiece. I'll tell you all about it after while."

Pecos lay back with his eyes closed, but sleep was a long way off. His mind kept sorting the hints he'd received. He was now quite certain that neither Cole Addis nor Ed Roe was the top man in the business. It was a matter of scope. This was bigger than highway robbery. He had a hunch they were out to bankrupt the McCabe Company, another hunch someone was out to control Butte City, and through that the mines of The Hill.

Big Jim was snoring, but he knew by the frequent complaint of bunk boards that Hernandez was as wide awake as himself.

"Butch," he said.

"Yes, Keed?"

"What do you think of Butte Hill?"

"Those four-beet silver mines? Poof!"

"If the Northern Pacific ever gets rails through this country, those four-bit mines as you call 'em might go up to a dollar."

"Listen to me. Gold . . . that is good. But silver . . . I will tell you about silver. In Chihuahua, my uncle Bolivar García de Santiago Fuente, he own the silver mine. Plata Grande, so he call it. Now, to work the mine which is the biggest in all the Conchos River country, my uncle used *peones,* half to dig the ore and half to grow food, so that all the labor costs him nothing. The powder for blasting, the mules, the steel . . . these he receives free from the Army through good connections in the government. Only for the arrastres must he buy a little quicksilver, and yet at mining silver has my Uncle Bolivar gone flat broke and must flee the country for his debts. No, *Señor* Keed. If they dig silver on Butte Hill, then I say . . . pack up and go, for the town is a ghost camp already."

"Hear they hit sooty copper on the four-hundred-foot level of the Anaconda."

"Copper? What fool talk is thees? Rather would I have one silver *peso* than two pounds of copper." He leaned out of the bunk so he could look down in Pecos's face while he talked.

39

"Listen. In Miles City there was a tinhorn selling stock in London and Butte Consolidated Mines. Today is thees company bankrupt like my Uncle Bolivar. Always the big stock issue, big talk, and poof! Rather would I invest my dollars in the bonds of the Confederate States of America."

V

"The Big Take"

During the easy days that followed, Pecos found the road agents to be a careless, lawless lot, apparently little different from the run of men one would find at some roundup camp. An exception was Owen Peck, a swaggering, adenoidal man who claimed twelve notches for his low-slung guns. And then there was The Turk, who was not a Turk but a Negroid Spanish Indian, massive and squat with gold rings in his close-set ears; and there was Mutt Frye, a drunken, filthy little man who bragged about the dead men who dotted his back trail.

Each morning one could sit and hear the distant cracking of Owen Peck's guns up one of the gulches as he practiced draw and shoot, draw and shoot for fifty cartridges.

Pecos, sprawled in the shade of the bunkhouse, said to Orofino Johnny: "Hear him talk, he's so good he don't need that."

"He's nuts." Johnny had a nice, smiling way about him. He was just too lazy to work, and so he had become successively a gambler and a road agent. "All he talks about is killin'. All he thinks about. He'd rob coaches at a dollar a night, just for the killin' chance he gets. Me . . . once I get a six, eight thousand dollar stake, I'll quit road agentin' for good. Fifty dogies, a log shack, and a young squaw, that's all I'd want. Wouldn't even carry a gun. I ain't mad at nobody."

They all disliked and feared Owen Peck—feared him the way they'd fear a rattlesnake in the dark.

Each night a smudge fire burned to drive away the mosquitoes that hatched by thousands in the grassy overflow of some beaver dams down the valley. Pecos watched Owen Peck shamble toward the bunkhouse, and said to Hernandez: "He likes me."

"*Sí*. Always the beeg, buck-tooth smile. But does he smile at your back?"

"He's *segundo* to Addis and figures I'm pressing him. He'll take some watching, that one."

Cole Addis had gone somewhere. About sundown on the sixth day he came back. Passing Pecos on his way up from the corral, he said: "Come around after grub pile, there's something I'd like to talk about."

When Pecos went to see him, Owen Peck was slouched in a chair, grinning with his loose mouth, listening to some story Cole Addis was telling.

Addis stopped talking and, moving with big, easy grace, stood and got down a bottle of whisky and poured some drinks. He never did continue the story, if, indeed, he had intended to, for at that moment Tom Little clumped in, cursing, bringing with him the smell of horses.

He said: "That bay sprung a shoe, and the nail galled hell out of him. Now what'll I do? It takes a real horse to carry me."

With the exception of Big Jim Swing, Tom Little was the biggest man in camp.

Addis said: "Take that big dapple white."

"And get shot?"

"Oh, hell, we won't have trouble." He handed Pecos a drink. "In case you haven't guessed, we got something cooking. Wagon outfit. Swanson stuff."

Most Montana silver mines hand sorted their richest ore, sacked it, wagon freighted it to Salt Lake City, shipped it on by rail to San Francisco, and, thence, around the Horn by sailing ship to Swansea in Wales, the nearest smelter capable of removing the metal from its complex chlorides and sulphates.

"You got a smelter now?" Pecos asked him.

"To hell with the ore. McCabe's been hiding gold and silver ingots in those sacks instead of making express shipments by coach."

"You'll be breaking McCabe." When Addis shrugged, he said: "Ever hear of the goose and the golden egg?"

"Sure, but as long as the rich diggings hold out, we'll hatch new geese faster'n we can kill off the old ones."

If the Pecos Kid had wanted to carry a warning to McCabe, he wouldn't have had the chance. At midnight every man except the cook was saddled and ready to go. There was a slight delay while Chevalier and Jim Flynn came with a remuda of extra horses, and that was Pecos's first hint of the long ride they were in for.

Cole Addis, a fine figure on horseback, set out in the lead, traveling swiftly but not too swiftly, steadily, through mountains and, as the morning sun grew hot, through rocky, sage-covered hills.

They crossed the stage road. The rain of a week before had dried off. North of them, a fine haze of dust hung in the air. It was the train of ore wagons.

Addis stopped where the road twisted through ridge reefs of reddish volcanic rock. His plan was simple. The wagon train would be cut in half by some narrows, and they'd surprise the forward wagons while holding off the ones in the rear.

It was pitifully easy. Mules and drivers were tired after the long, dusty drag. Ore wagons, two in tandem making up each unit, were pulled by long jerking strings of mules. It scattered them, and, as some lagged while others went on, they became further scattered. When the attack came, the lead drivers knew what the firing was about.

Pecos rode back and saw one of the teamsters down on his face in the sagebrush. A masked road agent was just riding away. Owen Peck.

Big Jim had seen it happen. Cursing, he jerked his carbine from the saddle scabbard, but Pecos jerked it out of his hand.

"You see what he did?" Jim cried.

"Yes, but it's too late to help the teamster, and there'll be time to take care of Peck."

"I'll do it now." He was trying to get by, and Pecos kept turning his horse, crowding him into the rocks. "You get out of my way, Kid. I'll snap his neck."

Hernandez came alongside then and got hold of Big Jim's bridle, and they calmed him down. By then, with Tom Little bellowing orders, the teamsters were lined up, disarmed, rifles taken from the wagons. As darkness settled, the wagon train was moved forward three quarters of a mile to a cutbank drop-off where one after another the ore sacks were slit open, and dumped.

The work continued by the light of pitch torches. The Salt Lake coach rolled up, was stopped by four masked men, robbed, and kept waiting.

No ingots were discovered, and now it was apparent that Cole Addis hadn't expected any. Chevalier and a couple of others drove the mules off to be sold at the Idaho gold camps, a four-day trip across the mountains. The raid had netted little else of value.

One after another the empty wagons were rolled over the cutbank to smash themselves among massive boulders at the bottom. Still not satisfied, Addis had Mutt Frye waiting to set fires at half a dozen places along the broken heap as it accumulated.

At last, at midnight, they headed back. It was a relief for Pecos to get the mask and blanket off. He was tired. The whole business had left a rotten taste in his mouth. He licked his lips. They were salty from sweat, and he spat it out.

He noticed without turning that Cole Addis had ridden up beside him.

Pecos said: "Hell of a trip for no money. How much did you lift off that coach?"

"Watches, poor scratch. You need money, Pecos? I'll see that you get money. More'n you got off that coach you robbed in Bird Tail Gulch. This is big, Pecos, like I told you. All you need to do is take orders."

VI

"Buck-Tooth Rattlesnake"

The crew returned, groggy for want of sleep, gaunt from hunger. Cole Addis managed a side-of-the-mouth joke, limped stiffly to the ammunition room, unlocked it, and got out a couple gallons of Kentucky forty rod. The stuff, hitting empty stomachs, had an instantaneous warming, unsteadying effect on them all.

Addis didn't drink himself. He stood with one boot propped behind him on the split-pine bench that ran along the front of the square house, the perpetual cigarette dangling from his handsome mouth, one eye closed against the smoke. Behind him, a gangling figure with guns tied to his skinny legs, was Owen Peck—Fishface, they called him to his back, but never to his face.

Half an hour and five drinks later found Hernandez whanging his guitar and half the outlaw crew singing the endless, bawdy verses alternating with:

> **Before I'd live a cowboy's life**
> **I'd shoot myself with a butcher knife,**
> **I'd part my hair with a wagon wheel**
> **And die with cactus in my heel.**

Orofino Johnny came up behind Pecos, clapped him on the back, and said: "You better have another before it's all gone. This likker's all the pay we're getting."

"I hear different."

"Sure, you hear different and you hear the truth." He was loud. Whisky made him swagger. He was a good lad, but he'd never learned to keep his mouth shut. "You ever hear of old Daddy Christmas? If the stagecoach pickings are bad, old Daddy Christmas comes around. Daddy Christmas from Butte City. We do him a favor, and he does us a favor. . . ."

"Johnny!" Addis was no longer slouched. He'd moved away from the bench. He stood with his legs spread, his hands dangling, his shoulders sloped forward.

Orofino heard him and laughed. "Yep, old Daddy Christmas! What the hell? We all know what goes on here."

"Johnny!"

This time his voice had a knife-steel quality that cut through the fog of alcohol in Orofino Johnny's brain. He turned, recognized Addis's posture, the look in his pale eyes. He realized what was coming. He tried to jerk the gun at his hip. He was no match for Addis.

Addis looked slow, but the guns were there, in his hands, as though from nowhere. There was a fragmentary hesitation. Then they exploded in unison.

Orofino was knocked back. It was as if he'd been hit by a sledge. His gun had half cleared its holster. It flew in one direction, and he fell in the other. He was dead, slumped forward with one leg bent under him when he hit the ground.

Addis had moved back with the recoil. He stood against the log wall. Smoke strung up from the twin muzzles. There was no change in his face. His pale eyes missed nothing.

Men had stopped singing. There were shouted questions, then silence. Sight of Orofino's body stunned them.

Addis spoke in a clear, biting voice. "He talked too much. I don't want men around me who get drunk and talk too much."

Owen Peck had moved inside. Pecos could still barely see

him. He was waiting inside with both guns drawn.

Pecos turned his back and walked toward the bunkhouse, meeting Big Jim on the way down.

"Come along," he said. "We don't want any hand in this."

Pecos slept most of the day. He got up, walked barefoot to the creek for a drink, and went back to his bunk again. Hernandez was awake above him. He leaned out to say: "Did I hear right when Cole Addis said the tinhorns of Mescalero made *even money* bets who would be carried out when you met face to face? Can it be that you have grown slower through the years?"

"To hell with you." Pecos tried to sleep, but the picture remained—that backward bend of Addis's shoulders, the easy twist and lift of his hands, the brief hesitation, the twin guns blazing, all so casual and yet so deadly swift. Swift as he'd ever seen. He wondered and kept wondering whether he himself was that fast, whether he had ever been that fast.

He got up when the cook banged his tin bucket in grub call. Afterward, through long twilight, he sprawled by the smudge fire, slapping mosquitoes, listening to the lazy voice of a dirty, red-whiskered road agent called Tobacco-Mouth Billy recounting the doings of ghosts in the "ha'nted" houses back in Pike County, Missouri, where he'd lived "befoah the wah." It was the way time was divided in the lives of the men of the 'Seventies.

Owen Peck came and almost immediately men started getting up, stretching themselves, and wandering off to the bunkhouse. Only Pecos and Tobacco-Mouth remained.

Peck hunkered himself, picked at his big teeth with a grass spear, and tossed it away to say smugly: "Notice they all pull their saddles when I come around? They don't hanker to be number thirteen."

Pecos asked politely: "What do you mean, seh?"

"I mean none of 'em want to be the thirteenth notch on my guns."

"I doubt anything like that was in their minds. I'd bend to the belief that they just don't like the smell of snake."

Owen Peck froze a little. He was still smiling as he stood up. Flames, breaking through the green spruce branches, lighted his face, brought a gleam from the saliva at one corner of his mouth. Pecos still appeared indolent, but he'd turned a trifle, freeing the gun at his right hip. He kept picking up little bits of ground litter and tossing them at the fire.

The silence had grown rather tense. Then there was a boot thud of someone coming down from the bunkhouse, and Hernandez spoke with soft music in his voice.

"*Señor* Peck. Look. There is even now a rattlesnake behind your heel and you will be stepping on it."

Peck spun and looked down. "Where?"

"There!"

Hernandez carried his gun high, at the center of his abdomen, its butt pointed toward his right hand. He drew with a hooking, Spanish cross-draw—the draw that those Chihuahua aristocrats learn as soon as they are big enough to lift a gun's three pounds of weight.

The gun exploded as he swept it back. By darkness its streak of flame marked the course of the bullet downward. It struck Peck's left boot heel just as he was moving with his weight on it. It tore the heel to shreds and left him fighting for balance.

"One hundred *pesos!*" Hernandez cried.

It was a thing they'd done before. Pecos was on one knee. There was a laugh on his lips, a wild light in his eyes.

"Called!" Pecos drew and fired on the word, his bullet smashing the opposite heel, leaving Peck sprawled back on the ground.

Peck had instinctively drawn. At five steps it was an easy shot for Hernandez who blew the gun out of his hand. Pecos's next shot rolled the gun over amid a geyser of dirt, but in the darkness Hernandez's third bullet missed.

"Decision!" Pecos cried.

"Alas," Hernandez said sadly, "I am in your debt still another hundred *pesos*."

Peck was rolling on the ground, holding the hand the gun had been shot from, his teeth bared with pain. He had no wound, but the bullet, striking close to his hand, was like being hit by a hammer.

Men were stampeding down from the bunkhouse, but Hernandez paid no attention to them. Crouched by the fire with a little black notebook, he wet a stub pencil and painstakingly inscribed a figure, drew a line, added a total.

"Alas, has anyone been tail over teakettle in debt like your poor Hernandez? Debt, debt, debt . . . thees awful burden. Do you know, *Señor* Keed, that to you alone I owe in debts the sum of fifty-four thousand four hundred five dollar and seex beets?"

Pecos, watching the road agents, said: "You give me that gunpowder roan horse of yours, and we'll call it square."

"No. To the Gonzales, the Fuente, and the Flanagan is a debt sacred. Listen while I swear that thees moneys I will owe you to the end of time."

Cole Addis pushed his way through the crowd that had gathered. He saw what had happened, laughed, turned his back on Owen Peck, and said to Pecos: "I always heard that fellow was greaser-fancy with a gun, but he's started something now. Don't blame me if one of these days he isn't around when the supper bell rings."

"Thanks." Pecos raised his voice so he'd be sure Owen Peck would hear. "If he gets shot in the back, I'll know who to kill."

VII

"The Idaho Kid"

It was past midnight. The Pecos Kid awakened suddenly and sat up. He walked through the bunkhouse, amosnoring men, and stood in the door. He didn't know what had awakened him. It could have been some unexpected sound, or only a hunch.

A horse snorted, and then galloped around the corral. There was a slight thud as the gate pole was dropped back in place. Half a minute later he saw the rider leaving, darkly silhouetted against the mountainside.

It was Cole Addis. Someone was up there, waiting. He heard the single note of a voice, a hint of laughter, and the click of hoofs moving through shadow along the rocky trail, down the valley.

Pecos dressed, hurried to the pasture, caught his horse. He mounted and rode bareback for a mile.

He stopped. The night was cool and still. The moon kept emerging from among clouds and disappearing again. He let his horse drift along for another half mile, then he pulled in on the rope hackamore, realizing that someone was quite close.

Two riders, moving slowly, had passed below him. He had a glimpse through timber. One was Addis; the other looked dark and short.

They didn't reappear. Thinking they'd stopped somewhere at the foot of the slope, he dismounted, descended, but found no sign of them. Returning to his horse he saw the stranger, alone, striking farther back down the valley.

Three miles off, the trail would cross a saddle in the ridge. He rode at a hard gallop, across the valley, and straight up the ridge. There he left his winded horse and started down, digging his boot heels against the steep descent.

The rider was there, suddenly, right below him. Rocks dislodged by his boots spilled downward. The rider suddenly reined in, and he could hear a girl's voice: "Who's there?"

She'd whipped out a gun. Moonlight made a flash on one of the surfaces of its nickeled, octagonal barrel. It was aimed upward at him; the hammer was rocked back; her finger was clenched firmly on the trigger.

"Cole sent me." He said the first thing he could think of that would stop her from shooting.

Her hand relaxed a little. She was trying to see him. She was so close he could smell her perfume—the same perfume he'd noticed on Addis that first night. He got halfway to his feet, grabbed hold of an exposed root with his left hand and, leaning far out from the bank, grabbed her wrist.

She'd imagined herself at a safe distance. She didn't realize what had happened until he'd thrust the gun high. It exploded, whipping lead and powder flame over his head. Her horse pivoted in the narrow trail and lunged downhill. She fell, and Pecos, still holding her wrist, fell with her through ferns and tendrils to the trail.

The gun was gone. He lay, his weight holding her down, while dirt showered over them.

She was baffled for a few seconds, then she twisted and clawed at him with cat-like fury. He got hold of her hands. He forced them down, one at each hip, and held her while she twisted and kicked at him. Finally she stopped. She was sobbing through clenched teeth, from fury rather than terror.

Her hat had fallen off. Her dark hair had come loose and

lay in wavy masses about her face, over her slim shoulders. She wore a man's shirt—in the struggle its top button had popped off revealing a bit of white lace, and her breathing threatened to pop the other buttons off as she panted from the struggle she was putting up.

Still holding her wrists, he got to one knee. She wore trousers. They were made for a boy. They were too large around the waist, and they fit her too tightly in the legs.

He asked: "Who are you?"

"That's none of your affair!"

"Why were you up here seeing Cole Addis?"

She breathed and looked at him. She twisted her lips down at the corners. "Why shouldn't I?"

When Pecos looked at Cole Addis, all he could see were those pale killer's eyes. A girl might see something else. Addis was so handsome—so tall, broad, swaggeringly handsome.

He looked around, saw her gun, released her, and picked it up in the same second. It was a rimfire Army .32. He ejected the cartridges, and tossed the gun back to her. She was sitting up, rubbing her bruised wrists. She let the gun lie across her thighs.

"You're the Pecos Kid!" She laughed at the surprise on his face and said: "I know something else. You're the one who robbed that McCabe coach on Bird Tail Pass. Cole says you used to be a regular sky-pilot fighting on the side of the weak and shiftless, and now you've turned out to be a coach robber. What made you change?"

Pecos thought it over and drawled: "Why, I guess Cole was flattering me. I never looked up a man's church standing before I sided one way or the other. What Cole really meant was that he rode on the side paying the most money while I just took the side where I had the most fun."

The answer delighted her. She rammed the gun back in its

holster and stood up to face him. "You mean you've done all you have just for the fun of it?"

"Maybe that's a hard thing for you to believe."

"No, it isn't." She'd got over her anger. A new type of excitement filled her. "I wish I were a man. I do."

"All right, say you're a man. Then what?"

"I'd ride, and rob, and I'd throw it away. I'd travel from Canada to Mexico and back again."

"If you were a man, you'd do those things."

"Yes."

"Down in Deadwood I knew a gal that did them things anyhow."

"And I would, too. I asked Cole to ride with his gang."

"And Cole said . . . no, no, little girl . . . so you minded him."

He'd intended to bring up her anger a little in the hope she'd talk and reveal her identity, but her emotions lay primitively close to the surface, and she cried: "No, I didn't mind him. I could ride with him and rob with him any time I choose."

He waited for her to go on, but she'd checked herself. He said: "Well, why don't you?"

"You're daring me?"

He changed his tactics. He didn't want her riding back to Cole Addis and making trouble. "No, I'm not daring you."

She forked back her thick, dark hair and whispered: "You were. You were daring me. You don't think I'd have the nerve."

Three days passed. The Pecos Kid, returning through late twilight from a horse hunt up the valley, found Tom Little waiting to talk with him near the corral.

"Confab," Little said, jerking his head at the square

house. They walked up the path together. "Got a new recruit. Don't ask too much about him. Boss seems to be touchy."

"Thanks."

The door was closed, an unusual precaution on a warm evening, and Owen Peck lounged with a cigarette dangling loosely from his lower lip. His right hand was still bound with rags torn from an old shirt, advertising that it was sprained from having the gun shot out of it.

"How's the flipper, Peck?" Pecos asked with mock solicitude.

"It's comin' around."

Pecos laughed and followed Little inside. He closed the door with his heel and saw the new recruit seated in shadow by the far wall.

The girl. He should have guessed, but her being there came as a surprise.

She'd cut off her hair, or else she'd braided it and bound it tightly beneath her black sombrero. Hiding her forehead and nose was a molded, black silk mask. She wore boots, trousers, a shirt, and a beaded buckskin jacket. At first glance she looked like a boy, but it's almost impossible for a woman effectively to masquerade herself in cowboy's range clothes.

She saw Pecos and leaned forward; her lips were parted a trifle. He could see the throb of excitement in her throat. To hide any surprise on his face, Pecos leaned over the lamp and risked burning his cheek to get the stub of his cigarette lighted.

He said, talking cigarette smoke from the side of his mouth: "Who's your new man, Cole? The mysterious one all fixed up for some kind of masquerade ball?"

Addis didn't like the remark, and the lean set of his chin showed it. "The Idaho Kid wears a mask all the time. Any objections?"

"No-o. I don't give an unholy damn if your Idaho Kid goes around in his nightgown with dinglebobs on his toes. Well, what's up? Another ore train? If it is, you'd better spot me my shells before we start. I didn't get gunpowder money out of that last one."

Addis's big shoulders tightened the material of his shirt, then he decided to laugh. "What you been doing, spiking your coffee with vinegar?" He walked in his stiff, cowboy manner to the cupboard, got out three little buckskin sacks. They made a solid, jingling thump as he dropped them on the table. "Here's some payoff for you and your pards. The big cut's yours, but divide it as you want. Don't say anything outside. I haven't paid off everyone else yet."

Pecos held the gold pokes in his two hands appraising their good sixty ounces of weight. "Funny, I didn't see this heavy color come off the wagon."

"Neither did Orofino Johnny."

Pecos took the hint and let the matter drop. He sat with his boot heels on the edge of the table, hat shading his eyes, and listened while Addis outlined a plan for robbing a McCabe coach headed for Three Forks.

"If it was me," Pecos said, "I'd let McCabe rest for a while and take one of Ben Fillmore's coaches." From the corner of his gaze he noticed that Ben Fillmore's name made the Idaho Kid flinch. He went on blowing ash off his cigarette, examining the coal. "Yeah, I'd take on that Ben Fillmore." She didn't flinch that time. She was leaning forward, watching him. "I hear he's big shakes and growing bigger. Hear he's buying options on half the mines on The Hill. Out to control Butte like he controls Last Chance. Must be a man that rich sends something out on his stagecoaches."

Addis said with unexpected heat: "Fillmore's not in the gold exchange business at all."

56

"Maybe not, but. . . ."

"What you got on your mind?" Addis pushed himself back from the table. "If you got any idea about taking over this gang. . . ."

"I wouldn't be talkin' to you about it if I did."

Addis took a deep breath. "Well, maybe we will take on Ben Fillmore when we grow up to his size. But tomorrow it's the McCabe coach. McCabe keeps buying gold, and he gets it through. I have a hunch he makes a big gamble just once in a while, sending it out in the coach we'd least expect. So we'll take a look at that coach heading for Three Forks."

They left a couple of hours before daylight—those in the room together with Hernandez, Owen Peck, and Tobacco-Mouth Billy. At a switchback leading down toward the stage road, the girl managed to delay and come up beside Pecos who was riding last in line.

When the others dropped from sight over the rim, she said: "So you thought I wouldn't have the nerve."

"Why, you sure enough do have some influence over Cole."

His tone made her hands tighten on the bridle. She whispered through tense lips: "Maybe I'm in love with Cole. Maybe I'd follow him to hell and back. Maybe I'll just take off my mask, and let my hair down, and we can ride together, Cole and I. What are you laughing about, anyway?"

"I wasn't. I was just thinking. I guess you don't know what a rough bunch of boys they got holed up yonder. Six or eight of 'em are as tough as Cole Addis. They follow him now because there's always money to go around. But a woman like you is different. You don't go around. You belong all to one or all to another. That means trouble."

Their horses, jostling on the narrow turn, had brought

them close together. He seized her by the arm, turned her, and with sudden strength drew her hard against him and kissed her. He kept her there for a moment.

She twisted to get away. He held her. Then, when he turned her free, he found she was not struggling any more. She was breathing as she had that night along the trail.

She whispered: "He'd kill you if he saw you do that."

"Why don't you call him?"

"Maybe I will."

"Like you told him about meeting me before?"

She wheeled her horse then and rode down the switchback where Cole and the others had stopped to wait. She did not turn around at all but went right on.

VIII

"Deadfall"

The Three Forks coach was loaded with Army officers headed back to Fort Henderson after a celebration in Butte City. The coach did not even carry a strongbox, and the only express shipment was a bag of repair parts for a sawmill at Bozeman. Addis's hunch had been wrong.

The girl left them somewhere along the way. After a day in camp, Addis left, too. He returned from Butte, smelling of barbershop pomade, and immediately called Pecos, Hernandez, and Big Jim to the square house. McCabe, he said, was most certainly getting his major gold shipments out, and he wanted the three of them to spend more time in Butte to unearth how he was doing it.

In the meantime, he intended to stop the Salt Lake coach at Big Hole, just for luck. If anything they learned in Butte indicated that to be unwise, the gang was to be informed at Stonehouse.

They approached Butte cautiously, but there was no trouble. That night, when McCabe went to his office, after watching the arrival of his Benton coach, he found Pecos waiting for him.

"I'd begun to wonder what'd happened to you," he said, sitting down and looking at his big-knuckled hands. "You better do something pretty quick or there'll be no McCabe Company to pay you off."

"Hold tight for a couple more weeks. There's a big fat man

at the head of that gang, and he's trying to put you out of business. Who'd want to do that? Fillmore, maybe?"

"With the N.P. due to shove rails through here in a year, or two at the most, Fillmore wouldn't go to the bother. He's more interested in getting hold of those silver veins up on The Hill."

"They don't rob his coaches."

"They don't want to antagonize him. You got it in your head this is bigger than it is. You should have informed me of that attack on the wagon train. I'd have ambushed them and wiped them out."

"You'd have ambushed 'em and got a few, and there'd be more to take their place. Never any shortage of road agents. They got their eyes on the Salt Lake coach tomorrow, too, but a deadfall would get you nowhere. Just keep the gold off it. When the chance comes, we'll bust that gang wide open, but the chance isn't now."

There was someone outside the door. "Gloria?" McCabe said, and opened the door admitting his daughter. She was the same slim, blonde girl he'd glimpsed that first night. "This is the Pecos Kid."

"Yes, I know."

"He tells me the Lodgepole Gang is out to rob our Salt Lake coach tomorrow."

She cried: "Then we'll have something fixed up for them!"

"No," said Pecos, "you won't."

"Why?"

"They'll know who tipped you off, and I'll be a dead man with a couple of dead friends. And where'll you be? Any better off than before? I doubt it."

She showed her temper. "You're not telling us what to do!"

"No, you can do as you like. But if you're going to make a

deadfall of that Salt Lake coach, I want to know it now, because me and the boys'll be heading over the hill."

"You threatened that before," McCabe put in.

"It wasn't a threat . . . it was a promise."

He left with Pat McCabe's grudging assurance that he'd send the coach through the same as ever, but he kept watch the next day to make sure. It left with its usual load of passengers and one shotgun guard.

Returning to the hang-out, they found two-thirds of the men there, drunk and quarreling, with a dead man on his face near the corrals. Mutt Frye and a renegade named Joe Buffalo were holed up in the root cellar, and most of the others were shooting at them.

In a while the shooting stopped with a third of the men laid out from whisky, and the others gathered around a saddle blanket where The Turk took them on at three-card monte. The dead man, an Australian called Pink, lay forgotten by the corral.

Pecos came up and said: "You better bury him."

An Army deserter named Thomas turned and said: "If you want him buried, bury him yourself." Then he saw who it was, and it sobered him. "Oh, Pecos. I didn't notice."

"You kill him, Mutt?" Pecos cut in.

"He was askin' for it," Mutt said.

"Then you bury him."

Mutt got to his feet, cursing under his breath, and did as he was told.

Night settled.

Hernandez said: "You figure Cole will have his boys back tonight?"

"He might camp over at the Stonehouse."

At midnight Addis arrived with his beat-out crew—what was left of it. Pecos guessed what had happened the moment

61

he saw Addis limping up on his horse-stiffened legs.

Addis stopped and said: "They were waiting for us. Eight or ten guns at the crossing. Did you know about it, Pecos?"

Pecos stood with his arms dangling ready to reach for the guns at his hips. He said in a very low but very clear voice: "If you really believe that, the time to settle it is now."

For a second Addis seemed to be on the edge, then his manner told Pecos the danger had passed. "If I thought you knew, you wouldn't have the chance to go for your guns." And he limped toward the house.

Pecos could see Chevalier, Peck, Jim Flynn, and Half-Pint Corruthers down by the corral. He thought of the girl, and it made him sick. "Where's Idaho?"

Addis stopped and turned as though he'd hit the end of a rope. "What do you care about Idaho?" he barked. Then he toned down. "Idaho wasn't along."

At the house Addis told him that Dutch Hank and Quinlin had been killed, and Tobacco-Mouth Billy, wounded too badly to ride, had been left at the Shoshone encampment near Stonehouse.

Addis fixed him with a hard gaze and said: "How about that greaser pal of yours? I'd kill him if I thought he got drunk in Butte and talked too much."

"He didn't know you were hitting that coach."

Two days later Tobacco-Mouth got to camp, hanging onto his horse, with a story of escaping from a roving group of Bannack vigilantes. More was heard of Bannack vigilantes before the week was over.

With Addis on one of his extended absences, four men under Half-Pint Corruthers, up to some private sluice robbery, were surprised on Coldwater Creek. Two of them were captured and hanged, but Half-Pint and a young fellow named Nealy escaped by riding to the stronghold and getting help to fight the Bannack riders off at Breakneck Ridge, five miles to the south.

When Addis returned, he'd already heard of the ruckus. He sent for them, but Nealy, suspecting what was coming, managed to escape. Half-Pint wasn't so fortunate. Owen Peck, firing from an arm rest between two poles of the corral, got him squarely between the shoulders as he galloped bareback up the trail.

Then Addis made a little speech. "Nobody's going to jeopardize the whole outfit for the sake of some two-bit sluice robbery. You all been getting paid. Now I have something big coming up. Something damned big. Maybe a couple thousand for every man in camp. How does that sound?"

That night Addis sat across the table from the Pecos Kid, a cigarette in his handsome mouth, and told him about it.

"I been in Benton. Got a line on McCabe up there. I was wrong about his gold shipments. He's been buying it and storing it. Now he's contracted with the Prentiss boat, Sioux Chief, to take three thousand ounces to Saint Louis, and I have reason to think he'll ship that much with Dobbs-Henderson, too. He'll sneak it out on one of those slow freight outfits to Three Forks, and up to Benton the long way around by the Judith Gap. Let's see . . . this is Tuesday. It'll leave Butte Thursday morning. We'll nail it on the other side of the pass sometime late Thursday night or early Friday morning. The outfit will be pretty well gunned up, and we just lost four men. Where's Jim Flynn and Chevalier?"

"Out on a horse hunt."

He laughed from the side of his mouth. "Out on a sluice rob, you mean. Find them for me, can you?"

"I can try."

He sent Hernandez and Big Jim to look for them and rode

to Butte City, The Hill among mines and prospect holes to the rear of McCabe's. There he waited for two hours for McCabe to return, and until long past midnight before he was alone.

McCabe's first words were in explanation of the ambush at Big Hole, saying it was his daughter's doing behind his back, but Pecos cut him off saying—"I'm alive."—and going on to tell about the attack Addis had planned for Thursday night.

McCabe looked blank and said: "I'm sending no gold on that freight outfit. I'm storing it, that's true, but I'll send it out by coach as the insurance company specifies once the trails are safe."

Pecos stood outside with the raw, sulphide smell of the silver smelters on the wind around him, suspicious of Cole Addis, suspicious of McCabe.

He had the sudden feeling that someone was cached in the shadow, watching him. His right-hand gun had come to his hand without him thinking. Still holding it, he walked warily, watching the plank corral. The horses were all bedded down. No alarm. It had been his imagination. No one had been shadowing him. He told himself that without being quite sure.

He rode back to the valley, getting there during the heat of afternoon. From the ridge he watched for a while. All seemed quiet. Monte game in progress by the bunkhouse. No one hailed him on his way to the corral. He turned his horse loose and started up the path. He noticed that every man at the monte game had turned to watch.

Alarm hit him like the buzz of a rattlesnake. He spun around. There was Owen Peck inside the corral. The same as when he'd killed Half-Pint. Rifle in one hand. The sun made a brassy shine on the breech plate.

Pecos walked on. The door to the square house was open. Addis, an indolent, graceful figure, was lounging there.

Addis spit out a stub of cigarette and said in his most pleasant voice: "Hello, Kid. Glad to see you back. Chev turned up right after you left. Guess you missed him. Come on in."

He hadn't seen Hernandez or Big Jim. Their favorite horses weren't around. He kept walking, knowing they could kill him any second they wanted. He went inside. The door hid his back from Peck's bushwhack gun. Sun flicker danced in his eyes. He realized that Addis wasn't alone. There are some men you don't have to see, and filthy Mutt Frye was one of them.

He was seated with a sawed-off double-barreled shotgun in his hands. Mutt said: "Right at your belly, Kid. Ten chunks of number two buck. You get the latigos loose on them Colts and drop 'em so I won't have an excuse to saw you in half."

Pecos didn't ask what was wrong. He knew.

The two men watched him unbuckle his belts, saw the heavy holsters swing around his body. He let them thud to the floor.

Addis tilted a chair against the wall and regarded him with cold-eyed amusement. "Well, Kid, I hear you paid a visit to Butte last night."

"Yeah. I saw McCabe."

"What about?"

"I wanted to get a job gunning on that wagon train. It'd be handy for us."

"Sorry, Pecos. You haven't got the cards to bluff with. You're busted. Out of the game. You were the one that tipped them off about the Salt Lake coach. You should have pulled your ticket pin and drifted. You were at the end of your luck and didn't know it."

Pecos recognized the futility of argument. Addis wasn't the type you talked out of things. He was no fool.

"Why didn't you have Peck shoot me in the back like he did Half-Pint?"

"I'm not hot-headed, any more than you. I left that far behind me along the trail. If you were worth one cartridge more dead than alive, I'd have killed you. I didn't, and that means it's the other way around. You're worth more alive."

"Why?"

"Don't get suspicious, Kid. You'll find out in time." He got up and walked to the door. "That is, you will unless you make Mutt spatter your insides around the room with that old double."

Addis didn't trust him alone with Mutt, for Owen Peck ambled in a couple minutes later to slouch in a chair by the wall.

"Where's Hernandez?" Pecos asked.

"That smart greaser?" Peck laughed with a slack sag of his jaw and spit in the direction of Pecos's boots. "You don't know where the greaser is? Remember to ask Cole when he gets back."

Cole Addis didn't return until almost dark. He smelled of fresh evergreen, so he'd been riding in the hills. Back of him was a half-breed flunky carrying a couple dishes of venison stew, one for Pecos and one for Mutt Frye.

Pecos discovered he was ravenous. He ate half the plateful, boiling hot as it was, without pausing. Then he blew, and said: "Where's Hernandez and Big Jim?"

"Been wondering if they're worth more alive than dead, too? Sure they are. They're earning their keep. Sent 'em on a job of coach robbery." Addis smiled and added: "Fillmore coach, just like you suggested."

"Deadfall?" Pecos whispered.

"No-o. Not wham-bang from the cottonwoods like you fixed up for me at the Big Hole crossing. Not that kind of deadfall. I'd rather have them taken alive."

"So that's it. You'll let the Butte vigilantes hang them."

"Not if they're smart, and not if you're smart. Why, Pecos, you three still got the world by the tail. You can still ride over the hill with a straight neck and no leaks. What's more, you can do it with some jingle in your pocket. The old heavy color. All you got to be is a little bit smart."

"Maybe you're getting some fun out o' talking in circles."

"I'd like to tell you, Pecos, but that's not my job. There's a fellow in Butte City, that's his job. You eat up, and we'll have your horse saddled. We're ridin' there now."

IX

"The Big Boss"

It was late, but there was still no dawn light in the sky. After long, hard riding they jogged through Butte's outlying cabins. Addis was in the lead with Pecos's horse on a lead string, then Frye with the sawed-off across the pommel, and a cautious thirty feet in the rear rode Owen Peck.

Addis drew up between a stable and the abandoned shaft house of a silver mine and said: "Let's have the blindfold now, Owen."

Pecos made no comment as a black silk neckerchief was bound tightly around his eyes.

Peck said: "You try to pull that off, and I'll bend a gun barrel over your head."

They rode past one turning and another, entered an alley, passed open doors from which poured the sounds of saloons and variety houses. These sounds ended. They rode for a minute through a portion of town that seemed almost deserted, then they stopped, and Addis said: "All right, here it is."

Pecos dismounted with Mutt Frye holding him by an arm. He was led through a door, up some deeply carpeted stairs, along a hall until the pressure of Frye's hand stopped him.

Addis rapped at a door, and said: "It's me. I got him along."

A voice that was an unfamiliar, deep resonance said: "It isn't locked. Come on in."

68

Pecos could see light around the blindfold. On the air were the odors of good cigars and good whisky.

"Oh, you blindfolded him," the voice said. "That was hardly necessary. I'm not anticipating trouble with Major Warren."

Pecos said: "I left that Major behind in 'Sixty-Five. We'll just let it be the Pecos Kid, if you don't mind."

"I don't mind."

Pecos pulled off the blindfold. He saw before him a man of fifty, short, bald, and fat, but with an intelligent face and a manner that showed he was used to command.

"You're Ben Fillmore?" Pecos said.

The man nodded, and they shook hands. Fillmore's grip was unexpectedly powerful. "I regret this show of force, but it was your reputation that made it necessary. Did Addis explain the situation to you?"

"I understand that Flanagan and Jim Swing are out robbing one of your coaches, and that it'll be a deadfall."

"Deadfall? Well, it will contain some duly elected officers of the law, but, unless our plans miscarry, no one will be hurt. Your friends, of course, will be taken in the act of robbery, and it would be in the power of Judge Cullabine to order a trial, but I doubt things will get that far."

He started looking around the room which was a combination parlor and office, about twenty feet square with heavy furniture. After pawing several drawers, he shouted: "Matthew! Where are those depositions that Krause drew up for me?"

A thin, gray man entered through some draperies and cat-footed to a sideboard where he picked up a big, bulging envelope. He handed this to Fillmore and left without a word. Fillmore took from it some documents, unfolding the top one.

"This is for the Mexican. Yours is one of the others, but they're all substantially alike. Notarized, witnessed, all they lack are the signatures." Thumbing to the last pages he chuckled and said: "You are even, I see, represented by counsel."

"Mind if I look?"

"Oh, by all means."

The deposition consisted of six minutely penned pages held by clasps along the top. A glance at the opening sentences of paragraphs told Pecos that it was a detailed confession.

I, Hernandez Pedro Flanagan . . . employed by Patrick F. McCabe, and The Three Forks Freight and Coach Company for the purpose of terrorizing competing stage and freight lines, especially the Diamond Bar Mercantile and Freight Co., and the various properties of the St. Louis and Montana Bank, or any other property of Benjamin W. Fillmore . . . did on the morning of July 18th feloniously stop the Last Chance coach near Corkscrew Turn on the Deer Gulch road for the purpose of. . . .

Pecos leafed on. The remainder of the deposition took the form of questions and answers, purporting to be put to Hernandez by a pair of lawyers named Krause and Woolsey, in the presence of a magistrate, Judge Andrew Cullabine.

He whistled a fragment of a tune through his teeth, and said: "Well, I'll be damned!" What looked like admiration showed in his eyes, but his mind was fixed on the fact that the deadfall had not yet been accomplished, nor would it be for a couple of hours, and, if he had his freedom and a good horse, there might yet be time. He said: "There was some mention made of rumuneration. You'd be giving us enough money to get out of the country?"

"Certainly. You'll find me practical in these matters. I thought perhaps two thousand for you, and a thousand for each of your pals."

"I assumed it'd be more." He was thinking it would make little difference to Fillmore, because once the papers were signed the lives of the three wouldn't be worth a Confederate two-dollar bill, anyhow. Killed, trying to escape—that would be it. "Mister Fillmore, seh, you'll be wanting us to get a long way off. You make that eight thousand instead of four and let me divide it. Then I'll deal. After I see the boys, of course."

"You'll sign now."

Fillmore's tone made Owen Peck shift his position. He stood, leaning against a leather-upholstered chair, his thumbs hooked in his cartridge belts. Mutt Frye had the sawed-off in the crook of his left arm. Addis was beyond a heavy mahogany table.

"Sign it?" Pecos said, his voice sounding loud in the dead quiet room. "I want to read it over first. All the way."

He discarded the two top depositions and took the third. The room was lighted by a three-burner kerosene lamp suspended on a counterbalance from the ceiling. He moved around so the light would shine on the paper. In doing it, he passed behind Fillmore. It seemed natural enough.

Still making no sharp move, he seized Fillmore by both arms, pulled him tight, and held him with his left arm crooked around his throat. Fillmore's hands were free. He tried to claw his way loose. He tried to cry out, but the sound was pinched off in his throat. His right hand pulled his coat open. A gun was there, strapped high, gambler-style, in a holster between his shoulder and his belt.

Pecos had expected the gun, but he hadn't known where it

was. He let go with his right hand, grabbed Fillmore's wrist, and the two reeled against the wall.

It had all taken only a couple of seconds. Cole Addis shouted a warning to his two gunmen not to shoot, and tried to get around the table, but, in turning, Fillmore had rammed the table, knocking it in front of him. It delayed Addis a couple of seconds, and by that time Pecos had the gun.

It was a European revolver of peculiar shape with a long trigger pull and no visible hammer. Pecos was baffled for an instant, seeking the correct grip. He dragged Fillmore along the wall, using him as a shield.

From the side of his gaze he saw old Matthew charge into the room clutching an old time Navy Colt in his two hands. Pecos was a perfect target for the old man. He had no choice. With quick power, he flung Fillmore in that direction and fired at the suspension chain of the lamp.

With his own gun he'd have hit it, but the strange revolver's self-cocking mechanism threw him off. A bullet tore past him. He fell away. The room rocked with concussion. He could feel the burn of flying powder. He was on hands and knees in the table's brief protection. From there he fired again at the lamp, hit the brass counterweight, sent the lamp clattering to the floor.

The chimneys were gone, but one of the wicks still burned. "The door!" Addis was shouting. "Forget that and cover the door." Pecos swung his arm in a horizontal arc and tried to reach the draped doorway through which Matthew had entered.

He rammed against someone. The unexpected impact sent him reeling. He found himself against the wall with velvet drapes under his hands. He groped. Powder smoke filled the room. It strangled him. He set his teeth, held his breath to keep from coughing.

He found the door. A light burned in the next room, but

the drapes kept him from silhouetting himself. He slammed the door, and someone fired, driving splinters after him.

He was in a rather long, narrow room filled with ledgers. A row of windows along one side were covered by bars. He had to keep going. He lunged through a door and realized, too late, that he was in a sort of vault.

He started to turn back. He stopped with a trapped-rat feeling. By dim light he saw a heavy oak door almost hidden by some filing cases. He dumped the cases out of the way but found the door locked.

He saw a bolt and pulled it. The door was bolted on the other side, too. He stepped back and drove his weight, shoulder first. The door held. He drew back again, and checked himself as he heard a rattle on the far side. The door came open. Beyond lay a hall in semidarkness. He flattened himself in the door, expecting a red blaze of gunfire.

Nothing happened. The hall seemed deserted. Then he caught the scent of perfume. Her perfume. She must've opened the door for him. He looked for her, but she wasn't there any more. A bracket lamp burned around a turning, and there were the stairs.

He took them four at a time. The thick carpeting snagged a boot heel, and he fell. He rolled to his feet, his body against a door. He reached, opened it, and saw Owen Peck come in sight at the head of the stairs.

Peck took the first step before checking himself. He had a gun in each hand. He realized that Pecos was there and no longer running. He'd have dived for cover if he'd had a chance. The walls hemmed him in. He lived a long time in that fragment of a second with his face turned sick and slack from fear.

He fired both guns, but Pecos, aiming from the waist, was a quarter second ahead. The European gun threw a heavy bullet. It hit Peck and smashed him backward. Peck's guns lashed the opposite walls, cutting plaster that rattled in a shower like stones.

He almost sat down, then his knees buckled, and he caved in at the waist, propelling him forward. He slid on his face, flopped over and over, ending head down, arms wide, on his back within two steps of the bottom. One of his guns lay at Pecos's feet. Pecos snatched it up. It seemed good to have one of Sam Colt's pieces in his hand again.

"Owen?" Cole Addis shouted.

Addis had been running. When no answer came, he stopped. "Owen!" he called in a different tone.

Still watching the stairs, Pecos retrieved the other Colt, unbuckled Peck's gun belts, strapped them on.

He could hear men shouting deep in the house. He backed outside. It was getting light. The scene was not what he'd pictured it. There was a large, Eastern-style stable, some plank corrals. He started that way and saw the saddle horses tied beneath an ornate little open-sided shed.

He untied all of them, led them around the barn, around the corrals, down a terrace to a placer-pockmarked bench of Silver Bow Creek. A bullet struck the ground and screeched away, chased by the sharp pound of explosion. He was out of sight a second later, hidden by a high reef of gravel.

There he took time to look at the horses. It would be a long gallop to Deer Gulch where Hernandez and Big Jim were waiting for that Last Chance coach, and it wouldn't hurt to swap his weight from one horse to another along the way. He chose Addis's big gray, and turned the other two loose.

Startled by the gunshot, a meadowlark veered, came to rest, and burst into song. It was a fine morning—if William Calhoun Warren, the Pecos Kid, had been in a position to enjoy it.

X

"Corkscrew Turn"

He rode straight across Silver Bow, through ponds and trailing heaps, past the Star of the West smelter, through suffocating white smoke where ore from the hard-rock mines lay in long heaps mixed with pine logs, burning week after week, breaking down the primaries, producing a dirt that could be handled by the charcoal blast furnace.

His trail sloped upward along the base of the mountains. Sulphur and arsenic from the roasting fires had already burned off every blade of grass in the great cup of the mountains that held the town. The evergreens had turned brown and dropped their needles. After a long climb he was above the smoke haze, and the air smelled good again. He stopped and let his horse breathe. His eyes, narrowed and intent on the trails from town, picked up moving figures, horsemen— two of them, then three, then two more, all on the gallop.

He watched them turn up the stage road. Even at a mile through the haze, he recognized the erect figure of Cole Addis, and the short, stooped lump that was Mutt Frye.

The three or four minutes' rest had helped. He decided not to swap his weight to the gray. He reached the stage road and turned along it as it made long, climbing loops along the mountain, then through the steep rock slash of a gulch toward the Continental Divide.

Dawn was red. He kept going. Each time he looked back, they'd be there, closing the distance. It had been a hard night for the buckskin, while they were mounted on fresh horses from Fillmore's stable.

Midway on a long, straight climb a bullet stung the rock ten feet above his head and was chased by the sharp crack of explosion. His experienced ear told him the gun was about three hundred yards away. He couldn't allow them to gain on him further, and yet the Divide was still more than a mile away.

He couldn't swap horses here. He spurred the buckskin to a gallop as more bullets pursued him. Back of him six riders were strung out, forcing their horses. A seventh man had dismounted and was on one knee, aiming and firing a rifle.

Even when the distance increased to four hundred yards, the man kept arching the bullets in, hoping for a chance shot that would wound one of the horses, or frighten them, make them falter.

The road swung inward to a feeder gulch and back again. It brought his pursuers suddenly a hundred yards closer, across and below. Mutt Frye, getting his horse stopped, was bent double, pulling a carbine from the saddle scabbard.

Shooting from the ground at that range, Mutt could kill him. Pecos drew and fired. The bullet was close enough to send Mutt's horse in a rearing circle, then the ribbon turn that had carried them close put them at a distance again.

He could tell that the buckskin was about run out. The animal faltered but kept going. Stopping here would be suicidal, but the road plunged from view beyond a shoulder of rock about two hundred yards up the gulch.

Pecos talked to the buckskin, urging him forward. It took the guts out of him to be cruel to a horse. He kept talking, watching the rock shoulder, watching the men behind him.

At last he was there. The sharp turning hid him. He slid off, turned the buckskin free, tied the gray to some washed-out roots of a pine tree. With a gun in each hand, he aimed a volley down the road, driving men off their horses to scramble to any cover they could find. The answer came in a hail of lead that pounded the rocks in front of him.

Pecos mounted and rode again. It was a quarter mile to the next turning. No sign of them.

It was easier going now, and the gray was comparatively fresh. A high valley lay beyond the Divide. There were groves of timber. The grass was lush green up here, removed from the sulphur smoke.

He stopped to let his horse breathe. He dismounted to listen. No sound of pursuit. Momentarily, at least, he'd outdistanced them.

He had a general idea where Deer Gulch was located. Corkscrew Turn, the deposition had said. He'd have to play his luck. The stage would be due in half an hour, so the barricade would be up.

At a sharp turn he saw that a five or six hundred pound piece of slab rock had been levered out to the middle of the road. He turned his horse. A solid green wall of forest stood above, but he knew that men were crouched up there, looking down on him.

"Hold!" he heard Hernandez say. "It is heem, the Pecos Keed."

Pecos said: "All off, boys. I got that from the big boss himself."

He turned the gray upward from the road, belly-deep through fern and buckbrush, over deadfalls that crumpled brick red under the hoofs.

Men showed themselves here and there—Big Jim, The Turk, Tobacco-Mouth, and powerful Tom Little with an Eight Gauge shotgun in his hands.

Little was covering him. Little *knew*. He knew that the coach was a deadfall.

"Put that gun down, Tom," Pecos said softly.

"I'll put the gun down when I get good and. . . ."

Hernandez had swept his gun from its turned-in holster at the same instant, as though the action were automatic with Pecos's words. "¡Sí! Covered . . . and I do not become happy when forced to shoot a man between the shoulder blades, Tom."

Little stiffened. He lowered his gun, dropped it to the ground.

Hernandez, with a laugh in his voice, said: "Like the old saying of the *gringos,* he who throws the gun away lives to run some other day. Now, Keed, tell me why you have run that gray pony until he is covered with lather like he is in a barber-shop."

Pecos sat with one of Owen Peck's guns in his hand and said: "They're sendin' a deadfall coach up here. Bent to her hubs with deputy sheriffs. Jim, pick out three likely horses. Our days with the Lodgepole Gang are finished."

XI

"The Big Squeeze"

Pecos found McCabe and sat down, dropping his hat on the floor. "Fillmore." He said the name with a wry twist of his lips as though he'd have spat if there'd been moisture enough in his mouth. "That's our man . . . Fillmore."

"What in the devil are you talking about?"

"By the way, does Fillmore have a daughter? Twenty years old, pretty, put together like a young Gypsy?"

"You mean there's a man in the territory not damned well aware he has a daughter?"

Pecos laughed and rubbed his stubble of beard with a tired gesture. He'd been a long time without rest. Fatigue was heavy as quicksilver in his muscles, and, when he closed his eyes, little bluish lights danced in them. He kept thinking about her. She was old Ben's daughter, and she had saved his life. "What's her name?"

"Dolly. Child of his second marriage. He's had four wives, you know. Like a Turk he is about wives, only making them wait their legal turns. Dolly's mother was an entertainer. Singer on the river packets, and in the dives of Vicksburg before the war. She's like her mother, from what I've heard. What about her, lad?"

"Why, I'd not be here if it hadn't been for her." He didn't enlarge on it. He went on, talking in brief sentences, telling everything that had happened since their last meeting.

Pat McCabe, after hearing the story from Pecos's lips, sat

79

with a face that was gaunt and tired. "So he's the one! Yes, I'd suspected Fillmore's out to be king of the territory. He'll end with fifty million, a captain of commerce and industry. Another Leland Stanford. He'll own all of Montana."

"Whoa! Don't let him get any bigger."

"I know what I'm talking about!" McCabe's voice had a saw-blade twang that carried through the walls outside. Then he checked its volume but not its intensity. "My stage and freight line is just something to kick out of his way. That isn't what he has his eyes on, and it isn't this town. It's *The Hill* back there. You think that's just another group of silver veins, don't you? You think silver is poor scratch?"

Pecos, laughing cigarette smoke from his mouth, said: "I like gold better because I can carry more in my pocket. Of course, silver is good stuff, too, but. . . ."

McCabe silenced him, saying: "Silver be damned! Do you know anything about mining?"

"I know a heap more about cows."

"Well, listen. There are several millions lying up there in the silver bonanzas, I suppose, but these deposits are all what a miner refers to as *secondaries*. They accumulate near the tops of the veins and play out. Four hundred feet down in the Anaconda do you know what they struck? Sooty copper and so damned much of it that it makes Spain's Río Tinto look like a bag of pennies. And not just the Anaconda . . . you get deep on every one of those veins and. . . ."

"Long way to ship copper ore . . . Swansea in Wales."

"Ever hear of the Northern Pacific railway? They can refine it here as soon as they get that sort of transportation."

"Seems like the N.P. is having a hard time getting past Bismarck."

"It'll be here, next year or the next. Villard is reorganizing.

Maybe he'll go broke again in Fort Keogh, and, if he does, he'll reorganize a third time. And when it comes, it'll make Butte the biggest camp in the West. Anaconda will be the biggest copper mine in the world."

Pecos had heard it all before. He'd heard the same thing in Central City, and Oro Seco, and Tombstone, and none of them looked like New York. That's how it would be with Butte when the silver bonanzas played out. But in the meantime he was working for McCabe.

"All right, Mack, so it's the richest hill on earth. I'll take your word for it. How does Fillmore get it by destroying you?"

"He already controls the Diamond Bar and the Hellgate lines. When I'm gone, he'll have the final say on every road, and every wagon. Find out how easy it is to ship to Swansea at a profit *then*. Oh, he'll be clever about it. Maybe he'll hold the present rates on blasting powder, tools, smelter flux. Maybe he'll raise the price of food to push up the price of labor. He'll give them the slow squeeze, extend credit, buy in one after another. I don't know what he'll do, except that he'll have The Hill when the N.P. gets here."

Pecos got his boots down from the table and said: "Then, seh, it looks to me like it's up to the independent operators to keep you in business."

"Try and convince them of it," he said bitterly.

"Why, yes. That's what we'll do."

"How?"

"Suspend operation. Get your outfits off some place. Haul between Benton and Miles City. Let Fillmore think you're all through. I was watching him last night, the way he paced the floor. Other folks never move or talk fast enough to suit him. There's more pounce than 'possum in Ben Fillmore. You quit hauling for two weeks, and I'll wager he'll be strangling the bald-headed old hell out of those operators on The Hill."

"I'm not suspending."

"Why, that's up to you, seh."

That evening, while Pecos was passing his time in a small poker game at the Green Front, he heard that a print dodger was up on the express board, announcing the last runs for McCabe coaches to Salt Lake City and Fort Benton. So he'd changed his mind.

Butte City showed no immediate effect. Pecos killed time. It was hell, being in town with nothing to do. Women, gambling, and whisky all attracted him, and to keep out of trouble he got a job trimming ore at the Galway Mine.

For one who was made ill at ease by the four walls of a room, the black bowels of the earth were unendurable. He quit and was seated in a Chinese café when Jim Swing found him.

"You got to come with me, Kid. You got to stop that crazy greaser."

"The hell with him. Sit down and have a piece of pie."

Pecos knew that Hernandez was out on a whoop-up, and as always this big, tow-headed saddle tramp was trying to keep him out of trouble. Right now there were big furrows of worry in Jim's forehead, and he had the eyes of a bereaved cow.

"You know what he's done? Got into a ruckus with Spade Hartman over a girl down at Hungry Annie's, and now he's challenged Hartman to a duel. Hartman's got that whole Missouri Gulch crowd at his back, and they'll kill him."

Pecos ate pie and said: "Hartman has a notch for every man he's killed filed in the stocks of his guns. A man like that doesn't have friends. He has houn' dogs that follow him around ready to bite him when he's down."

"You know how Butch is when he's got that guitar under one arm and his gut full of liquor."

He was almost in tears. Pecos felt sorry for him, so he made his voice tougher than ever. "What can *I* do? Look what happened to McKetrick when I tried to save him from that Hole-in-the-Wall bunch . . . he challenged *me* to a duel. I should have fought him. Sometime I will. I'll shoot my initials in that Spik-Mick's hide and show him who's boss."

The duel didn't materialize. At the last moment Hartman discovered an urgent desire for other scenery, departing on the Hellgate coach, leaving Hernandez in undisputed charge at Hungry Annie's and Missouri Gulch.

About six o'clock in the evening two days later Pecos was in his room at the London House changing clothes for a supper invitation to McCabe's when the door opened and Hernandez dragged in.

Pecos said: "Well, ruby red eyes, you look like you been out on a dandy."

Hernandez sat down, held his head in his hands. "*Amigo*, I have fallen into days of ill fortune. I am in poor health and far in debt. Please lend me the sum of four hundred dollar that I may buy medicines and pay my honest debts before I am arrested for defrauding an innkeeper."

"The hell with you."

Pecos looked at him without sympathy. He had a two-day crop of whiskers. His mustache needed trimming. His clothes were sagging and dusty. A barber had days before dressed his hair with an overdose of pomade, and now a thick mop of it hung greasily over his forehead. He exuded an aura of wine and cheap perfume.

"Where's your guitar?"

"Eet is broken. Some fool stepped on it while doing the

polka in a dance hall, and it is beyond repair. Oh, *madre mía,* look across the long miles from my beloved Chihuahua and see what has happened to your poor wandering boy thees night. Behold him, seek and bankrupt, without three dollar in his pants and even the friends of his heart speet on heem when he ask for four hundred steenking dollars."

"You owe me fifty thousand already."

"*Sí.* But more. I am a man of honor." He moved to get the little black notebook from his hip pocket, and leafed halfway through. "The sum is feefty-four thousand, seex hundred twelve dollar and seex beets. Debts of honor, *señor!* Listen to me, Hernandez Pedro Gonzales y Fuente Jesús María Flanagan, while I will never forget it but go on owing it until the last day of time."

Pecos gave him two hundred and told him to sober up. He had little trouble with liquor himself, but he kept getting deeper and deeper into the poker games. To keep out of trouble, he got Hernandez and Big Jim and made the long trip to Fort Benton, a center for steamboat traffic on the Missouri. Returning eleven days later, he found that the Fillmore squeeze was on in earnest.

Food prices, which had slowly been declining for six months, had suddenly leaped upward. There was still plenty of lean Texas beef, but flour was $60 a hundred, Utah spuds were $30 a bushel, and eggs a dollar each. Miners, no longer able to buy grub at the old wage scale, stayed off The Hill, and the Sons of Irish Freedom, calling it an English plot, paraded all the way from Dublin Gulch to the Travona where they rioted with a group of Cousin Jacks, and blood flowed, though not fatally.

Three mornings later an organizer for the secret society of Molly Maguires was found hanged to the sheave timbers of the Rising Star Mine at the head of Beefstraight Gulch. Dark corner talk all blamed a tough employer, Lloyd Siddons, owner of the Transcontinental Lode, and the Maguires struck back, setting off an underground powder magazine that closed the main working entrances to the Transcontinental indefinitely.

Next week it became known that Siddons had optioned the Transcontinental to Ben Fillmore, and sold outright his interests in the Blackjack and the Plata Fina on The Hill.

Most of the operators kept going, raising wages a little, trying to squeeze out a margin of profit, but another jump in food prices brought pay demands that almost shut down the camp. Even placer miners in the gulch, hiring coolies at two dollars a day, felt the pinch.

Miners demonstrated in the street and somehow found money for whisky. After hours of speech making, they tramped downhill toward the big, clapboard warehouses of Fillmore's Diamond Bar Mercantile, singing:

> **In every sort of season, whether it's wet**
> **or dry,**
> **I toil for me livelihood or lie in the**
> **street and die;**
> **Oh when me pockets jingle, I live on**
> **lager beer,**
> **I'm a rambling wretch from Erin's sod,**
> **The son of a gambol-eer!**

Reaching the warehouse, they found the door wide open and supplies being carted to the platforms and stacked out for the taking. When the excitement quieted, Ben Fillmore came out on the roof and made a speech.

Did they know, he shouted through his cupped hands, that a single ton of high grade *silver glance* ore like they were taking from the Black Hawk, the Plata Fina, and a dozen other mines, would pay the day wage of a hundred of them? Did they know that McCabe's Three Forks Company had plenty of mules and wagons to haul food from Benton, from Salt Lake, or from Fort Walla Walla, if need be, but that it had suspended operations after a conference with those silver kings of The Hill?

"Why?" shouted Fillmore, "why? Are they out to mine silver, or are they out to drive the Irish and Cornish away from Butte so they can bring in a horde of Dagos from Chicago? I don't know what you gentlemen think, but *I* think it's high time the Irish and Cornish stop fighting each other and turn their attention to their real enemies. Did I hear someone say, Fillmore has an axe to grind? Well, by heaven, it's true. I have an axe to grind. Because the same combine that is trying to drive you from Butte is trying to bankrupt me."

It was a great speech. They marched away, loaded with grub, cheering Fillmore and damning the silver barons of The Hill. But all the shouting and marching did no good. The mines remained closed. One after another the roasting fires died. For the first time in many months the air was clear, and a man could breathe without the rotted garlic fumes of sulphur and arsenic biting at his lungs.

Some men left for a new silver camp in Idaho; others formed a party and walked eastward to the Yellowstone to build a raft and float downstream to Bismarck where the Northern Pacific was once more hiring labor. But most of them stayed on, broke, idle, ready for violence.

Big Jim Swing narrowly missed being killed when someone hurled a pickaxe at him from the doorway of The Shamrock. It had reached the point where no mine owner or anyone identified with the McCabe interests dared approach Dublin Gulch or Butte itself closer than the head-frame of the Neversweat shaft.

At that point McCabe was able to get most of the independent operators together for a meeting at which they agreed to hold tight against further encroachment, but Fillmore, chiefly through options, already controlled better than forty percent of The Hill. However, the meeting was only half a success, as McCabe was unable to get either of the smelters to pledge shipments from their large store of silver bullion, so the freight line remained suspended.

Fillmore increased his freight tonnages only a little, supplying about half the camp's needs. Wildcat outfits rolled in from Benton, Hellgate, and Salt Lake City, but road agents terrorized the trails to an extent unknown since the downfall of the Plummer gang making them demand doubled and treble rates.

Fillmore then played his next card, reopening the King Midas Mine with fifty miners at high wages, and posting a sign at the foot of the Steward dump saying he'd put on six hundred more if he was not prevented by tunnel restrictions on the part of the Silver Barons Association.

Feeling ran high. All day men were gathered around the sign. In the afternoon, Fillmore agitators organized a march up the hill where they were met by gunfire from detectives on the Garflock property. The miners, armed for the most part with pick handle shillelaghs, retreated, carrying dead and wounded with them. The funeral parade proved to be a fighting rally, and there was buzzing along the new telegraph line to the territorial capital in Helena.

Fillmore didn't relish the intervention of troops. He went to work quelling the thing he'd nursed along. He hastily hired a brass band that all afternoon and night played Irish airs in front of The Shamrock, knowing that not even the most warlike member of the Molly Maguires could move from the sound of it.

Riding in from the west after sunset, the Pecos Kid drew up at the brow of The Hill and listened as a few instruments of the band played and a hundred voices were raised in an excellent, untrained symphony.

With a cheer for bloody Cromwell,
They led him to the gallows tree,
Another murder for foul England
Another death for liber-tee.

Eight members of the association were sitting around the Silver Strike tool house, gloomily contemplating the news that one of their members, Otto Bleyhouser, owner of a group of claims along the north flank of The Hill, had optioned his holdings to Fillmore for sixteen thousand dollars cash and a quarter million to be paid, half in six months, and half in two years.

On the following days there were more defections—small owners who were willing to grab a good price and get out. After all, the Northern Pacific railway was a long time coming.

XII

"The Gun Play's the Thing!"

Pecos was at the corrals when Big Jim and Hernandez arrived from the Bitterroot, driving a herd of mules. They were joking about old times when they "took the lid off Denver," as McCabe came up and said in a voice that dampened their good spirits: "It hasn't worked. It's been a damn' failure. I shouldn't have suspended operations. I should never have listened to you."

Pecos looked gaunt from sudden temper, but he controlled himself. "Maybe you're right. It's gone further than I expected. I never realized a bunch of Irishmen could cause so much trouble."

"Hungry men!" cried McCabe who was Irish himself. "Have you ever been hungry and had the gate of your livelihood slammed in your face?"

Pecos thought about it and reminisced: "Never forget one winter down on Wind River, it was twenty below with snow three feet deep and me without grub. I got so damned hungry I boiled and ate the buffalo skin teepee I was living in. That was a tough old bullhide teepee, too."

Hernandez said: "On the rancho of my uncle, José Santiago Santos Bolivar y Santa Ana Gonzalez, was there a foreman name Pancho who for three months lost in the desert ate rattlesnakes, picking his teeth weeth the fangs, and a finer man you never knew, but afterward the *caballería* had to shoot him, he was so mean."

"These Irish aren't mean."

Hernandez, dropping his Spanish accent as he was perfectly able to do when he chose, said: "Sure, and it was as me dear father said . . . they're the salt of the earth."

Pecos asked McCabe's estimate of the amount of silver bullion being held by members of the association there in Butte and received an answer of half a million ounces.

"We can't run those freight wagons out of here empty," Pecos said, "and it'll be hard getting consignments from merchants up in Benton, road agents being what they are. But here's something to consider . . . last I heard from Benton, flour had fallen to twelve dollars a hundred and no takers. Those outfits are feeling the Fillmore squeeze, too. But if we could get them to ship that bullion, and we could use it in Benton as collateral, we could make a killing. Put every horse, mule, and wagon into one convoy. If we could roll that through both ways, and repeat a couple of times, prices here would hit the skids. We'd have his hold broken."

"Yes, and what will *he* be doing all the while?"

Pecos laughed and said: "Why, all we have to do is find *that* out, and we'll have him licked."

That meeting of the operators proved more successful than either of them expected. Lloyd Siddons was there. He'd returned from San Francisco to collect a ten thousand dollar payment on Fillmore's option on the Transcontinental Lode, but the money wasn't forthcoming. Fillmore had stalled behind a legal technicality, and now Siddons wanted them to back him in retrieving his property.

McCabe cried: "You mean Fillmore lacks ten thousand cash?"

"He's overreached himself. Times are tough since Jay Cooke went under trying to finance that streak of rust they call the Northern Pacific. I was in San Francisco, and I know. You can't get a dollar in call money even for the Comstock, let alone a camp called Butte they've hardly heard of. I tell you, Fillmore has reached the end of his rope."

By the end of the meeting more than one hundred thousand ounces of silver bullion was pledged for the big shipment.

Riding night and day, horseback to Helena, and thence by coach, the Pecos Kid made a journey to Fort Benton and back again. Returning to Butte, he saw that the Star of the West smelter had its charcoal blast going. Once more there was a haze from the roasting fires. A stream of rusty-looking water ran from the pumps that were unwatering the Anaconda. At ten or fifteen minute intervals one could hear the rush and rattle of ore as it was carried by metal-faced chute from the portal of the Neversweat to some bins behind the National Exchange. Only one man in four had a job, but credit was easy. Butte was suddenly its old, booming self again.

It was night. Hernandez limped inside the freight office after an almost continuous twenty-four hours in the saddle. He elbowed past some half-drunk mule-skinners and reached McCabe who was writing cash orders for advance pay good on presentation to the Territorial Trust in Benton.

"Where's Pecos?" Hernandez asked.

"At the Star smelter, checking bullion weights."

Hernandez cursed in choice English, Spanish, and Cherokee. He'd ridden within a quarter-mile of the smelter on his way to town.

"What's wrong?" McCabe asked, looking at his face.

"I have been to robber's roost. I have talked weeth. . . ." He stopped short of calling Chevalier by name. "Weeth a friend of mine. There will be old *diablo* to pay before those wagons reach Three Forks, *señor,* and all his legions of hell waiting to collect."

"We can match man for man everyone he has at robber's roost."

"Everyone he *did* have. But *now* . . . is there a gunman, or renegade, or so much as one saloon tramp left between Hellgate and Cheyenne after such a mob of cutthroats have been brought together?"

He limped back to his horse. Big Jim had seen him arrive and was waiting. They rode together to the smelter where Pecos, standing in deep boredom, hat low on his eyes, was writing down the ounce weights of ingots as they were weighed on a balance big enough to take a man.

He kept jotting the figures, called out while listening to Hernandez's story. He said: "Sure you can believe what Chevalier says?"

"He hates the yellow insides of that gunman, Addis. Besides, did I not count forty-two men myself?"

"How many did Chev say?"

"Seexty-five, seventy."

"And they'll pick up Fillmore's private rough boys here in town. We'll play hell fighting off a hundred men when that convoy gets strung out in the mountains."

"Then it is all off?" Hernandez asked sadly.

"I didn't say that."

Hernandez flashed his white teeth in a grin. "Ha! Then the Pecos Kid has sometheeng up his shirt sleeve."

"Only my arm, and it's getting almighty tired pushing this pencil."

It wasn't the truth, but Pecos had learned that the Spanish Irishman had never quite mastered the art of keeping his mouth shut. He left Hernandez to complete the silver inventory, sent Big Jim to the freight house to keep check on the stock and wagons, and walked down the steep streets toward the Fillmore mansion.

It was a huge, three-story, brown, shingled place of squarish cupolas, bay windows, and ornate iron bric-a-brac standing in the center of some big grounds where shrubbery, imported from England and Pennsylvania, stood bare of leaves despite the repeated coatings of wax that were supposed to make them proof against the smelter fumes. It was past midnight, but lights were still burning here.

He didn't bother to climb the stone fence and attempt to conceal his approach by passing through the shrubbery. He walked directly through the rear carriage gate, past the coolie house, and the barn. A lantern burned in the barn, and a shadow moved. Pecos stopped as a chipmunk-faced man came to the door with a brush in one hand and a currycomb in the other.

"Fillmore around?" Pecos asked.

"Yeah. I was just wiping down his horse."

"How about Dolly?"

"I ain't seen her."

He walked on. He didn't know whether the hostler suspected anything. Back somewhere, in the depths of the carriage house, men were talking, laughing, rattling money. There were others around. A horse jerked with a jingle of bridle links. A voice he'd never heard before was saying: " . . . well Stallcup did it without a quirt or anything. He'd take this big bay and. . . ."

The voice drifted off. Through the back door screen he could see the stairs down which Owen Peck had sprawled with a bullet through him. He followed a mosaic wall around to the side. A door there was locked. He kept going, passed beneath an arbor bare of vines, and tried the front door.

Light from a suspended lamp shone down on him. He looked quickly around. The hall was empty. At his left were the main stairs, covered with Persian carpet. At his right were some sliding doors that lacked half an inch of being closed. He moved close, fixed his eye, and saw a large drawing room furnished with baroque magnificence. No sound, no movement.

A board creaked, and he spun expecting to see someone on the stairs. No one there. He noticed his gun was in his hand. He dropped it back in the holster. It had been someone on the second floor.

He thought of Dolly more than her father, the man he had come to find. He owed his life to her. That made his job all the tougher.

He climbed the stairs, wondering if he'd meet her. It was impossible not to think of the way she moved and talked, of the warmth of her hands, the slim conformation of her body. He reached the top of the stairs. Inside, the house proved bigger than he'd imagined. He turned to his left. There was a sunroom with a bay window looking out on the grounds. Then he saw the massive, oaken door she'd opened to free him from the vault.

He listened at Fillmore's office. Fillmore's deep voice came to him, and the reedy tones of old Matthew. Pecos touched the knob, turned it little by little, making not the slightest sound.

Then a third voice came to him, and his hand froze on the knob. It was the voice of Cole Addis.

"I could quote your own words on that score, chief," Addis was saying. "*Don't overestimate a friend or underestimate an enemy.* Don't underestimate the Pecos Kid. He's more than any ordinary cow-walloper or gunman. He was smart enough to be a major under Johnston in the War Between the States."

"I'm not underestimating him," Fillmore said smoothly.

"I just don't intend to send men out there that I can't trust in order to increase their numbers. Anyway, according to my figures, there'll be thirty-nine, and that should be sufficient."

Pecos had a sudden feeling that someone was behind him. He spun around. The hall was empty. Sweat ran down his cheeks. The heat in the house seemed insufferable. He'd never been at his best inside four walls. He was like Big Jim. He'd spent too much of his life under the open sky.

He walked back along the hall and found a place of concealment beneath some stairs leading to the third floor. He hunkered and wished for a cigarette. He anticipated a long period of waiting, but a scant five minutes passed before Cole Addis, Ed Roe, and a stranger came out and went clumping down the back stairs.

Pecos, puffing an unlighted cigarette, was at Fillmore's door before they got outside. He opened it and went in.

Fillmore sat beyond the mahogany table *scratch-scratching* on paper with a little ivory pen, hitting the ink with a blotter as he went along. Without looking up he said: "Matthew, I do wish you'd. . . ."

He stopped. Something made him realize it wasn't Matthew. He looked up and stiffened when he saw the Pecos Kid.

"Hello, Mister Fillmore," Pecos said politely. "No, I wouldn't get my hands out of sight. Guns aren't your strong point. Handling money you'd have me down to my last *centavo* in five minutes, but guns . . . now that's a different matter. Every man to his game."

He walked around the table with Fillmore's eyes following him and glanced in the next room. Matthew wasn't there. No one had seen or heard.

He pulled the lamp down on its counterbalance and lighted his cigarette off the chimney. Fillmore stared at him.

He seemed unable to get his breath. His cheeks were spots of scarlet, and he was white around the lips. "What do you want here?"

"You, seh."

He stared at Pecos. It was hard to tell whether fright or rage had the upper hand with him.

Pecos went on in his smooth, rather lazy voice: "You're coming with me. Without giving alarm or causing trouble, you're coming with me. Now get your hat."

Fillmore lunged to his feet. His stomach rammed the table, and his legs almost knocked his chair over backward. His fists were doubled. The size of his stomach made him stand very erect, and at that moment he resembled a bantam rooster, but there was nothing comic about him. He was still the man who had faced an angry mob and sent them away cheering.

"If you think you can get away with a thing like this . . . !"

"You're talking too loud, seh."

Pecos, with a brushing movement of his hand, drew the Colt from its right hand holster and rammed it hard in Fillmore's side. The man inhaled sharply from pain. Sight of the gun made his cheeks lose color. Pecos knew how he felt. He'd had his own insides tie up in a knot when he looked into the muzzle of a gun. "I'll have your gun." He took it, another European piece, identical to the first. "It seems almost like I'm collectin' 'em."

Fillmore, looking at the Colt, got words through his throat: "Shoot me and you'll never get out of here alive."

"Why, maybe not. Neither of us. That'd be bad. Take your hat. Put it on. Take that walking stick, too. Now go ahead of me. I'll be keeping the Colt out of sight all the time, but it'll be ready, Fillmore, seh. If we meet anybody, just speak. If anybody asks questions, say we're going yonder to talk about freight. Otherwise, s'help me. . . ."

Filmore whispered, short of breath: "All right."

They went to the hall, down the front stairs, outside. Laughter and the voices of men came from back toward the barns. Fillmore heard them and looked sick at his helplessness to summon help when it was so close.

"Across the yard. Swing the stick and act happy. The play, seh! *The play's the thing.* I was snowed in one winter with a prospector in those hills back o' Yellowjack, and he had a set of books. Shakespeare. Fellow in one of 'em said that. *The play's the thing.* By the way, what sort of bush is that, Mister Fillmore? That one with the silver bark? I hear you paid two, three hundred dollars to get some of these things from England. I bet they thought they'd died and gone to hell when you unpacked 'em in this arsenic smoke."

"Where are you taking me?"

"Wagon ride. On that convoy headed out to Benton. It's fine in the mountains this time of year, away from the smoke and the hullabaloo."

With an effort, Fillmore managed to laugh. "Say, one has to admire you. Taking me out of my own house, from under the noses of a dozen gunmen. What are you doing, working for that McCabe outfit, anyway? You should be with me. What is he paying you?"

"Sorry, Fillmore. Table stakes. I'll stick to the side I came in on. That's why I'll die broke. No genius for money."

"You have no regard for your neck, either. I'm too influential in this territory. You can't kidnap and murder a man like me and get away with it."

"You won't be harmed in that wagon convoy. Not if it isn't attacked. You'll get to Benton as safely as it does. In fact, that's why you're going along."

He called Big Jim to the darkness of the stable runway,

told him to get Fillmore out of town to the third stage shanty seventeen miles out on the Three Forks road, then, with dawn silhouetting the horizon, he walked back to the mansion.

XIII

"Little Gypsy Hellcat"

Lamplight and tobacco smoke streamed from the open door and windows at the far side of the carriage house. Pecos could hear voices, familiar and unfamiliar, the creak of movement, the jingle of coins. A man in the door moved to make way for him.

"Cole around?" Pecos asked quietly.

"Yonder," and he jerked his head.

Pecos stood in the door. Eleven or twelve men were seated and standing around a square table watching as The Turk, with a pack of cards almost lost in his huge, blackish hand, dealt with what seemed to be clumsy slowness. Cole Addis stood with one boot propped on a box. He saw one of the men catch a jack that made three of a kind, grunt, and toss in his cards. Then he looked up and saw Pecos.

He went rigid for just an instant, then a smile turned the corners of his mouth. "Well, I'm damned. There's old vinegar guts himself! *Guts is right.* Did you come down here all alone, Pecos?"

Mention of the name Pecos stopped the game. For a few seconds there were no sounds except the uneasy floor and chair creakings as men moved to slightly different positions.

Pecos said in his easy voice: "Why, I might be alone. What difference does it make?"

"You were a spy out there at the valley, and I don't like spies. To my way of thinking, the best place for a spy is six

99

feet under ground. Only I doubt we'll go to that much bother with you."

"I doubt whether you'll shoot me at all." His tone made Addis listen. "Before any of your boys go for their guns, you better check with Fillmore. Oh, I know, you were just talking to him . . . you, and Ed Roe, and another of your boys, but things have just recently changed."

Addis's eyes were slits above his high cheek bones. "How in hell do you know so much?"

"Why, I was there, waiting my turn. I was inside, talking with him, before you got down the back stairs. He's a reasonable man, Fillmore is, when he sees the strength of the other man's arguments. In this case, I convinced him he was making a mistake. So he says to tell you the attack is off. That's what I came to say."

Without taking his eyes off Pecos, Addis addressed The Turk: "Go up to the house."

Pecos said: "If you're looking for Fillmore, you'll have to go a heap farther than the house."

"Are you trying to say you kidnapped him?"

"I wasn't going to use that word. I just convinced him it would be better for his health if he got away from all these smelter fumes. Offered him a free pass to Benton . . . on the wagon train."

Addis cried: "If you're holding him on one of those wagons, why we'll take him off!"

Pecos had a slow way about him. He looked around at their faces, drawn and suspicious under the lamplight. "That's up to you. But the first man that rides up to a McCabe wagon is going to draw a lead bullet. If Fillmore gets shot in the ruckus, who's going to pay you off? I ask you all to think that over. *Who's going to pay you off?*"

He knew there was a man behind him. A gun, in being

drawn, always makes a certain *click-click* sound. The rattle of its cylinder. Without turning Pecos said: "Cole, you tell him to put his Colt back in the leather. I'm pretty certain Mister Fillmore wouldn't want anything to happen to me."

Addis took a very deep breath, steadying himself. Then he said through tight lips: "Put it back."

The man was Tobacco-Mouth Billy. He lowered his gun, grunted, spat, and rammed it in the holster.

"Why, good mawnin', Billy," Pecos said, and walked away up the flagstoned carriage track to the steep street.

The wagon train had been scheduled to leave at dawn, but the stock was wild, some of the drivers were inexperienced, and most of them had taken on a pint or two against the rigors of the trail. They were still in the yard, trying to get in line, as the sun rose.

At about ten o'clock a volley of gunfire ripped through the excitement, and every man in the yard dropped his work to see what the ruckus was. They discovered that guardsmen hired by the independents to patrol The Hill had tangled with Fillmore men reinforced by some of the more irresponsible Molly Maguires. It was a pointless, drunken row, and, when both sides retreated, a dead man lay on his back in the middle of Kilarney Lane. No one seemed to know which side he'd been on. But it didn't matter.

It was past noon when at last the wagons were maneuvered into line, and the command was given that sent them one following another downhill, across the flats, on the first leg of the long haul to Three Forks and Benton.

Pecos had a drink of old Kentucky with McCabe. Both of them felt good to have the thing finally under way. Afterward he washed in water from the trough spout and walked, dripping, to the room he'd fixed for himself in the freight building.

He hadn't left the door closed, but it was closed now. It occurred to him that Hernandez had been there in his absence. He opened it with a wet hand and stopped a single stride inside with the realization that Dolly Fillmore was there somewhere, waiting for him. Her perfume was very strong. He blinked his eyes, trying to drive the sun flicker out of them.

A gun hammer clicked, and she said: "Come on in."

He made his voice good-humored. "What if I'd rather not?"

"You know the answer to that."

Slowly things took form. She was seated on a stool against the far wall, leaning forward, holding her .32 rimfire revolver in both hands, her hands resting on her knees, her knees pressed together. She wore a blouse and a riding skirt. Her face seemed thinner than he remembered it. It seemed to be all eyes, and the eyes were fastened on him.

"Come in," she whispered through her teeth.

"All right. I'm in. Now what?"

"Close the door."

He did, using his heel. The only light came from one smoky windowpane now. He could barely see her, but her eyes had had ample time to become accustomed to the gloom.

She said: "Where is he?"

"Your father? He's not here. You can see that. There aren't four men left in the freight yard. If that's why you have the gun on me, I'm warning you you're wasting your time."

"I asked where he was."

He needed some time to think about things. He didn't like the way she pointed that gun. He could feel water running down his neck. He said: "Mind if I dry myself?"

"I asked. . . ."

"Sure, and I'll answer. I reckon he's somewhere on the wagon train."

"He isn't. I was in here and heard you talking to McCabe. He's at Number Three cabin. I heard you say so. Turn him loose."

"All right, it's seventeen miles off, but. . . ."

"Stop!" Her hand had tightened on the gun.

He said: "Well, what can I do? I can't free him staying in this room, and I can't go outside."

The fact her father wasn't right there at the freight house evidently came as a surprise to her. She hadn't even suspected it on overhearing mention of Number Three cabin. Words came through her teeth: "I should kill you!"

"Dolly. . . ." He'd never called her that before. He licked his lips. "Dolly, they'll put him on the wagon train tonight. Nothing will happen to the wagons. He'll reach Fort Benton as safely as the wagon train does."

"His being on that train won't stop the attack?"

"You mean to tell me that Cole Addis would still cut loose knowing that Ben Fillmore might . . . ?"

"He can't stop them. There are twenty men out there under Mutt Frye, and nobody knows where the attack will come. How can they, not even knowing which road you intend to take? Pecos, you'll have to get him off that wagon train. You'll *have* to!" She stood up. The gun was still pointed, but her voice and eyes pleaded with him. She came a step forward, another. "Pecos," she whispered, "won't you do it for *me?*"

She'd saved his life that night in the house. Now he'd have to double-cross her. It was hell, but he had no choice.

She was quite close. She leaned against him, her cheek pressed against his chest. "I love him, Pecos. I love my dad. I know he's started a lot of rough play, but don't let anything happen to him. Help me, Pecos."

Her hands were soft and warm. They were around his neck. Her fingers tangled in his hair. Her lips were parted. Her skin gave off that perfume, but it was different when she was close, brought out by the warmth of her body.

He kissed her. It made him forget everything. It took him back over the raw, tough years, even before the war, when he was a kid, and there was another girl. That other girl—he'd almost forgotten her name, but for a moment it was almost as though she were here again, in his arms.

Dolly whispered: "Oh, Pecos!"

He got his mind free. No matter how he wanted her, he couldn't sell out the side he'd come in on. His lips formed the words: "Table stakes."

"What?"

The gun was still in her hand, the right hand that was around his neck. He reached, grabbed her by the wrist, and with a sudden twist snapped the gun from her hand. She spun away from him, quick as a mountain cat. She bent, trying to snatch the gun from the floor. He'd anticipated the move. He kicked it away. She was on hands and knees, still scrambling for it. He bent over, seized her by the arms, pulled her to her feet.

She fought. She clawed and bit. He held her at arm's length until she stopped and was sobbing and panting. He let her go. She held to the little rough-board table for support. Suddenly she saw her chance and darted toward the door. He let her get past, and seized her, holding her helpless with her arms behind her.

"No. You're not going to Addis."

Addis would know where to find Number Three cabin. Her mistake was waiting for him. She just hadn't realized the extent of the information she'd overheard.

He bound her wrists together with his neckerchief, tied her to the post of his bunk. He stepped to the door. The freight yard was empty. He called for McCabe, and then for Hernandez without getting an answer. At last, a hulking, half-witted hostler called Red Bub came to the door of a stable and stood with his mouth sagging.

Pecos sailed him a four-bit piece and said: "Get Hernandez and bring him here."

He went back inside. His hair was still wet from the bath he'd taken. He dried himself and paid scarcely any attention to the girl as she fought to free herself, and then called him names, every bitter, derisive thing she could put her tongue to.

Hernandez came on a half run and stopped just inside the door with his eyes popping at sight of the girl. "What is thees? Pecos, you have forgotten how to be a gentleman that you would keep a woman in your room by tying her to the bed-post?"

"Don't let your chivalry get the better of you. She's found out too much and has to stay here. You *keep her here.*"

"*Sí,*" Hernandez said sadly. "If it is your command, Keed, then she will be here."

XIV

"The Big Double Cross"

Dust in a fine, white cloud stood over the wagon train as it wound across the flats. The wagons were not strung out as was usually the case. Each lead team was kept close on the tailgate of the wagon ahead of it. Drivers plodded along with bandannas tied against dust that rolled upward from the wheels, from the hoofs, from everything. Guardsmen ranged the country on all sides, never going too far, never taking the chance of being cut off from the main group.

A short, truculent man had stopped his horse crosswise in the road, and sat with a sawed-off shotgun across the pommel of his saddle as Pecos rode up. He was Ned Comer, graduate of the Minnesota state pen, for the past two months employed as a company detective by the Silver Glance Mine.

"Oh, you!" Comer grunted, as though just seeing who it was. "That's a damned good way to get shot, riding up like that."

Pecos had never liked him. Straight through, the men on one side were as bad as those on the other. He rode on, past the long line of wagons, and found Fred Cluff up front. "Any trouble?"

Cluff shook his head. "There wouldn't be here. But once we're switching around the bends in the mountains, we'll be like pie at a Chink restaurant."

"We have some guns, too, you know."

"I wouldn't trust any of 'em. I wouldn't bet that half them

106

detectives on The Hill didn't have a piece of Fillmore cash in their pokes right this minute."

"You won't have any trouble."

He looked angry. "How in hell can you say that?"

"I didn't tell you, but you're going to pick up a passenger for Benton down at Number Three shanty. Ben Fillmore's going along."

"What the . . . ?"

"Big Jim has him there. He'll take care of him. If it isn't dark when you get to Number Three, wait for dark. Don't let your men know what's going on. Get Fillmore under the sheets of that big hooligan wagon, and keep him there all the way to Benton."

"Then what? How about those vigilantes in Benton?"

"Let me worry about them. And for that matter, you can let Big Jim worry about Fillmore. I don't think there'll be any attack on the wagon train."

He rode back through the heat of late afternoon. He dismounted into the shade of the pole awning in front of the freight office and looked for McCabe. He walked from room to room, and found the long building empty. No one near the corrals. Most of the gates stood open. Through hot, quiet sunlight he could see the haze of a million tiny gnats circling the corral earth.

He climbed some stairs up a steep pitch of the hill, went around to the door of his room. "Everything all right, Butch?" he asked.

After a slight hesitation: "*Sí*. Everytheeng."

He stepped inside. A shaft of sunlight cut the shadowed interior, and he saw Hernandez sitting beyond the table with a six-shooter in his hand. The gun was pointed very steadily at the Pecos Kid.

"What the devil . . . ?"

"Yes, you are covered, Keed." There was a tremble in Hernandez's voice, although none in his hand. He seemed ready to weep. "Keed, raise your hands and please make no trouble. I would not wish to be forced to shoot you down."

Pecos started to laugh. The intensity of Hernandez's dark eyes stopped him. The crazy Spik-Mick meant it. He could see the rest of the room then. The girl was gone. Hernandez had been packing things in his warbag.

"You damned fool, have you gone soft on that girl?"

"*Señor* Keed, you would not understand me. You have never felt the Spanish type of love. It is like a flame, like a forest fire, and nothing can stand before it!"

"Listen, you. . . ."

"Hands up! For her I would not hesitate to shoot. For her I give up honor, friends, everything. You must understand me, Keed. You must understand and not hold it against your poor Hernandez who must do what he must. This girl . . . she love me. She will sacrifice everything for me, and so must I also for her. Now, turn around that I may take your guns."

Pecos obeyed. He knew better than to make a fight. Hernandez was too good with a gun, knew all the tricks. He felt the weight of his Colts removed one after the other.

"Where is she?"

"Saddling the horses to fly with me, *mi amigo*."

"Where you going with her?"

"First to rescue her father, then we will ride into the sunset. Perhaps to Chihuahua where I will pay my debts and settle on the *hacienda* of my people. Time will cover the hurt, *amigo*. You will forgive your Hernandez that he has taken this woman away from you. You will someday come to visit and be received like a hero, like a great don, and sit at the table with my sweetheart who has grown more beautiful with the years, and with my children on all sides. . . ."

"You damned dumb Spik, she had her arms around my neck not five minutes before you came. And it wasn't the first time she had 'em there, either. How long do you think . . . ?"

"That is a lie!"

"Stop ramming me with your gun."

"A lie! You are trying to torture me. Only Hernandez does she care for, *señor*. With your guns have you won from me feefty thousand dollars, but at love will a Flanagan take the back chair to no man. She is mine, and so she will remain unto the end of time. And now, turn around and walk through the door."

"Where you taking me?"

"To the express house. To lock you in the strong room."

"What'll you do when you meet McCabe?"

"He is not there. I have sent him miles away to the silver smelter. I have sent the Chinese away . . . the half-wit boy I have sent away."

"You thought of everything."

"I have for three years had a good teacher . . . yourself. But now, alas, it is the time for *adiós*. But someday. . . ."

"Don't worry about us meeting again, Butch. We will. I'll find you. I'll find you if I have to follow you down the last snake hole in that Conchos River desert . And when I do, I'll put my brand on your hide. I'll put it there with a two hundred and fifty grain chunk of Sam Colt lead."

"Walk!"

Far below, Pecos could see men moving along the up and down streets. A steam hoist was laboring with a series of short whistle toots at the Anaconda Mine, warning a repair crew that a shipload of silver-copper ore would soon be rushing down the chute.

"Walk!"

The ore hit like thunder. Far across the flats he could see

the dust of the train but no wagons. They were gone, hidden by a ridge. The stables were deserted. The freight and express houses looked empty. Less than fifty steps away a woman was out, hanging up her wash, but she didn't look up, and Pecos couldn't call.

They walked through rooms that gave an empty resonance to the clump of their boots. The strongroom door was open.

"Inside!" said Hernandez.

Hernandez, a boot placed against the door ready to close it, paused a few seconds with the gun in his right hand, his left hand lifted in a sad sign of farewell. "Keed, someday you will understand. With tears in my heart, *adiós*."

"You lousy, yellow saddle bum. You dirty turncoat Spik-Mick. I save your hide five times, and this is how I get paid off. You sell me out for the first piece of lace that hitches her skirt at you. I'll find you, do you hear? I'll find you, and, when I do. . . ."

He found himself shouting at the closed door. He rammed it. It was locked. The room had no windows. It was dark as the five hundred level of the Anaconda Mine. The walls were thick pine logs, squared, and fit together tightly without a crack anywhere.

He kept cursing Hernandez. Finally he cursed himself out. He laughed, but there was no humor in it. He had a clasp knife in his pocket. He tried it on the plank door. He could carve his way out in thirty days.

He finally sat down with his back against the wall, found his makings, rolled a cigarette. He didn't light it. There was little enough air to last him through the long hours it might take for help to arrive.

About half an hour passed, although it seemed a lot longer. Unexpectedly there was a rattle of a padlock, and the door swung open. He lunged to his feet and saw Hernandez

110

Flanagan, standing in the opening.

"Don't say eet!" He put both hands in front of his face as though warning off a more bitter blow than he was able to endure. "She has double-crossed me . . . she is gone . . . she has made a fool of me. Was there ever on all the earth such a horse's end going north as your poor Hernandez? Pecos, *amigo* of my heart, take up a gun and shoot me, for I am a traitor."

Pecos went through the door and stood opening and closing his hands as though he wanted to get them on Hernandez's throat. "Where is she now?"

"How would I know?"

She had half an hour's start. She'd ride for help—or maybe she'd go alone, straight to Number Three cabin to find her father.

"Get my guns." Hernandez already had them in his hands. "Saddle the horses."

XV

"Strike Out"

The road from Butte City took a snaky, in-and-out course, avoiding the steep pitches, so Pecos and Hernandez left it after two miles to short-cut through the hills. Ahead, and to their right, was a dust cloud, fine as flour, gold-tinted by the sunset. That was the wagon train.

The hills steepened. There was scrub timber. They rode down a little gulch and came out on some flats with the cabin and corrals in sight. The wagon train had come to a stop about a mile away. Some of the wagons had pulled from the road, and the stock was feeding.

There was no one at the cabin. They rode on, urging their tired horses, and found Big Jim lying on a blanket twisting from pain while a teamster worked over a wound in his side. It was a bullet wound, still oozing blood. Apparently one of his ribs had been shattered.

Pecos grinned and said: "You fighting with women?"

Big Jim got his eyes in focus and managed to talk. "She sneaked up on the cabin. I was in the door, watching the wagons. She said she'd shoot me if. . . ." He didn't finish. The muscles of his neck were corded as the teamster probed around, packing the wound. "She did, too. She knocked me down with that little Thirty-Two. Rode off with Fillmore. I'm a hell of a guy, let a woman. . . ."

"And *I!*" cried Hernandez. "At least, she had a gun in her hand when she crooked her forefinger at *you*."

The wagon train stopped for grub and water. It moved on through early darkness. There'd be no real rest for men or horses until they reached the flats of the Three Forks a long night and day distant.

Pecos and Hernandez secured fresh horses from the corral and rode ahead of the train, up mountain slopes, through timber. After long, early darkness, the moon rose. They could see the road, far below, through the breaks in the forest.

Hernandez, long silent, said: "I could use a smoke."

"Go ahead, but hide the match in your hat." Pecos went on talking, giving voice to his thoughts. "You remember that ambush down on the Beaverhead? They'll pick a spot like that here, too. They'll try to cut the train in half."

"Perhaps the girl will not find them. Perhaps the attack will be called off."

"I wouldn't bet on it."

Hernandez rested one leg around the saddle horn and smoked, hiding the coal of his cigarette. Then with a quick movement he pinched the coal. There were riders through the trees, directly below them. One of them spoke. His voice seemed right beside them.

It was Tom Little. He was saying: "Why, yes, but Cole turned thumbs down on it. Then, when he heard that your dad was being held hostage, he called the whole thing off."

The voice of Dolly Fillmore answered: "My father ordered the attack! Cole had no business. . . ."

"Don't blame *me* for it, gal."

They said more, but the words were covered by distance.

Hernandez whispered: "We will have to follow them."

"Sure." Pecos sounded sleepy. "But we'll let 'em get up the trail a piece."

Hernandez fidgeted as though the saddle were too hot for

him, but Pecos seemed perfectly at ease, moving only to slap at an occasional mosquito. At last he nudged his horse into movement, down the rough hill to the saddle horse trail. "That's the trouble with you Mexicans," he said. "That's why you lost Texas. You got no patience. You always want to plant cotton before the ground's broke. That'll never work."

"Hah, we in Chihuahua are *caballero,* not jockeys of the plow. We are knights on horseback. Rather would we lose a piece of ground like Texas than make a living by leading black men in chains."

They'd been conversing in undertones, but that didn't rob Pecos's voice of its whiplash quality when he said: "Enough o' that talk, seh!"

"*Sí.* Enough. Tonight, I am greatly in your debt, but when I have made recompense, then will I argue weeth you for the honor of Chihuahua which is as great as the honor of Texas."

They rode on with Hernandez speaking his thoughts, addressing the night around him rather than the Pecos Kid. "Why is eet soldiers of the Confederacy have always one part vinegar and one part blood in their veins? In Chihuahua each alternate year is fought the civil war. If the Chihuahua Republicans lose to the Durango Royalists, is there hatred for ten years after? No. After the fighting comes big *fiesta,* and, when the *fiesta* is over, everyone has forgotten who won the war anyway."

They paused and sat listening for sound of the horses. They'd been traveling too slowly. They increased their pace. There was movement below, along the freight road. They had a brief glimpse, as the two riders turned up a gulch. The trail played out. They'd lost them.

Pecos said: "We'd better climb the ridge. Keep watch for the wagon train. I don't want to get more'n three or four miles ahead of it."

A cloud bank covered the moon, drifted away. They sat watching the road for what seemed to be hours.

Hernandez said: "In *Nueva Méjico* one time I owned a watch. It was a big silver watch with a key on a chain. I won it from a Chinaman playing three card monte, and, if I had it now, I would tell you how long until morning right to the very minute."

Pecos looked at the stars. They'd dimmed a little in the east but not at the zenith.

Hoofs clattered suddenly. A column of men came in sight and disappeared down the freight road. There were about twelve of them.

"That must be it," Pecos said.

He spurred away with Hernandez on his heels trying to keep pace along the unpredictable mountain trail. They found themselves outdistanced, pulled up to listen. On the air, carried by a night breeze, was the taste of dust—dust ground fine, stirred by the wheels of wagons. And a few seconds later came the crash of gunfire.

The volley was a sudden one, followed by a pause while echoes rattled around the high summits. Then the gunfire settled down to a steady exchange.

They kept riding, cleared a shoulder of the mountain, saw the wagon train strung out on both sides of a rock reef that ran from the summit to the cañon bottom. It was the Beaverhead technique all over again.

Teamsters had stopped and gone for cover. There was shooting from the wagons, from rocks along the road. Some of the guardsmen seemed to be making a fight of it, but most of them had evidently taken it on the lope when the fight started.

Pecos kept going downhill through pine thickets until the reef was a hundred yards away. He pulled in, grabbed

Hernandez's bridle. The two horses lunged in a half circle as their riders dismounted. Hernandez had both Colts drawn.

"See?" Pecos said. "There you are plantin' cotton before you break ground. Let's look it over."

They found one group of attackers scattered along the mountain, pouring a steady fire into the train, but the other group, the main one, was still silent, edging down in the cover of the reef.

"There's our meat!" Pecos said.

They opened fire, their four guns sending a sudden hail of twenty-four slugs into the unprotected rear of the column. It brought a mad scramble for cover. They could hear Cole Addis cursing his men, ordering them to make a stand.

Some of them did. Others, running, had exposed themselves to the rifles and shotguns of the teamsters. Organization vanished. Even those who first obeyed Cole Addis now stampeded in retreat.

Hernandez and the Pecos Kid found themselves hemmed in on two sides. The horses, frightened by gunfire, had drifted uphill. There was a nest of men ahead of them. They dived for cover as gunfire met them with a burst of flame.

Pecos lay with his face pressed in the rocky earth, reloading. He risked turning his head. He saw that Hernandez was forty feet uphill in the shelter of rock, also reloading.

Pecos cried: "Keep going! Get down to the wagon train!"

His voice brought a volley of bullets. They seemed to come from all directions. He edged along, not lifting his head, not lifting his shoulders, snaking himself, digging in his elbows. He saw his chance, raised, and dived to the cover of some rock.

"That's him!" he recognized Cole Addis's voice. "That's the Pecos Kid. Don't let him get away. Mutt, up the hill. Get behind that deadfall. That's his only way out."

There was a shotgun in Frye's hands. Pecos kept going, uphill, through rocks, around pine trees. The shotgun roared, but it was not aimed at him. It had fired in the opposite direction. It exploded again, wildly. Mutt lunged into sight and fell. He'd been riddled by three rapid-fire slugs from a six-shooter. Hernandez!

Pecos stopped. He realized Addis had been following him. He was coming around a pine thicket.

"Cole," he said. "Cole! Put your guns in their holsters."

Addis stopped. He stood tall, straight, broad-shouldered in a scrap of moonlight. He thought himself covered. He slowly thrust his guns away. Pecos moved a step, keeping his boothold on the rocky, grassy slope, and Addis saw him.

"Suppose those bets are still up in Mescalero?" Pecos asked. He looked careless. His hands hung at his sides.

"Yes, I suppose maybe they are." As he spoke, Addis went for his guns. He drew with a high lift of his shoulders, the draw that had spelled death for Orofino Johnny.

But this time he was not up against Orofino, and he knew it. He knew that the bets were down for him as they'd never been before. It made his hands and arms too tense. He tried to reach too fast, grab too fast, shoot too fast.

Pecos drew one gun. He drew with a hitch, a swing of his body, a pull of the trigger, all as careless as striking a match on the side of his pants. His bullet hit Addis and knocked him spinning. One of Addis's guns exploded. The explosion jarred it out of his hand. He caught himself and tried to come forward. He was bent over with his eyes staring, shocked and without focus. For a brief instant he'd realized what had happened, then his legs gave way.

Pecos rammed the empty cartridge cases from the gun and looked at him. He was dead; he was finished. For Addis, the end of the trail. Pecos should have felt triumphant. He didn't.

He just felt tired. He wished he could wash the sweat and powder smoke off his hands and face.

There was still a little long-range shooting, but the wagon train rolled on, creaking over the pass, brakes groaning down the western side toward Three Forks as the sun rose and grew warm.

Riding toward Butte at midday, Pecos stopped at Number Three cabin and found Big Jim sitting up in his bunk, building his strength on a thick, rare steak.

Big Jim chawed with one side of his mouth and cursed from the other. "No question of this critter getting here from Texas. He was too ornery tough to die. You hear about the U.S. marshal and the militia coming down from Helena? Well, they did, so those Molly Maguires will really have somebody to toss bricks at."

"When was this?"

"I dunno. That Injun mail carrier was telling me. He says the territorial governor sent 'em down to clean out The Hill."

"Maybe he wasn't getting his cut."

"Sweet name o' hell, is the governor a crook like Judge Cullabine?"

"I was just talking. I don't know anything about the governor."

He walked outside, to the corral, roped himself a fresh horse, tossed the saddle on him.

Someone was at the gate. He stood up, getting a kink from his back after tightening the latigo, and found himself face to face with Dolly Fillmore. She had the .32 in her hand.

He let a laugh jerk his shoulders and turned away from her saying: "If there's anything I'm tired of looking at, it's the muzzle of that popgun. If you hanker to use it, go ahead."

He put a boot in the stirrup, and stopped short of

mounting as she lowered the gun. She said through clenched teeth: "I *should* kill you."

He took his boot down, dropped the reins, and walked to her.

She said: "The militia has come to Butte."

"That's what I heard."

"On orders from the territorial governor. The gov hates my dad. He knows my dad has ambitions in politics. They both want to be Senator when Montana becomes a state. He'd do anything to put Dad in the wrong."

"That's out of my hands. I got nothing to do with territorial politics, and I don't own a square foot of The Hill."

"No, but you'd be the chief witness."

"Is that why you came here intending to kill me?"

"Yes."

"Why'd you change your mind?"

"You ought to know that."

Her tone was defiant, but her eyes weren't defiant. He kissed her. She clung to him, but with a gentle application of strength he pushed her away. She would have followed him, but he lifted her high and set her on the top rail of the corral. Then he mounted his horse.

"Where are you going?" she said.

"Yonder." He jerked his head toward the west, toward Hellgate, toward the Cœur d'Alene. "I'm ridin' a long way . . . before it's too late."

The Pecos Kid found a trail through the hills and followed it, through mountains and forest toward the boundless wilderness of the Bitterroot, the Snake River, the Columbia. It was mining country and timber country.

He'd travel for a while, then he'd rest his saddle, and send a message to Big Jim and Hernandez so they'd know where to find him. They'd have a nice little stake coming from McCabe. A man could take three or four thousand and do things with it here in the Rockies.

He stopped on a high divide. Mountains and timber lay as far as his eye could see, and after that the hint of more mountains and timber dissolving into purple. Without moving his eyes, he rolled a cigarette, drew out a match. The forest cover was dry for want of rain, so he put the match away and puffed the cigarette cold.

He was thinking that a man should never settle down and get married without seeing the country. He should see the country first, and get married on his way. That's what he'd do. He'd return sometime and marry that girl in Butte. And if not her, the one in Miles, or maybe that sweet little Cherokee quarter-breed he'd left in Wyoming.

Tamers of the Deadfall Towns

I

"Interrupted Journey"

They came on tired horses down the freight road. In the lead was William Calhoun Warren, the Pecos Kid, his lean body resigned to the saddle, his eyes almost closed against the bright Montana sun. Next was Hernandez Flanagan, dark and handsome, plucking a guitar as he rode, singing over and over the same lines of a Mexican border song. And in the rear, apparently asleep, was Jim Swing, a huge young man with blunt features and burlap-colored hair.

They'd left Frenchman's Shanties in Charlo Coulée at dawn. Since then they'd seen no human habitation, only the bare, browned prairie and the twin lines of the freight road.

At last they topped a low ridge and looked down on the Big Dry Crossing of the Missouri. Fifty or sixty freight wagons were in sight, unhitched, with mules and horses grazing across the bottoms. Some of the teamsters had pitched tents, or constructed wickiups, and along the brush were some teepees. The river, banks full from melting snows in the Rockies, followed a straight course between cutbank shores. There was no sign of the ferry.

Pecos drew up, took off his hat, and fingered his brick-colored hair. He licked the taste of salty alkali off his lips and spat before turning to speak to Hernandez Flanagan who still plucked the guitar.

"There it is, Butch. You better hide that Spik fiddle or one of those teamsters will shoot it to splinters, and you'll be making a new one out of cigar boxes like you did at Casa Miguel."

Hernandez grinned with a flash of white teeth against moccasin-brown skin. "They would dare? In all the history of my Chihuahua homeland there was never a man who won so many duels, who was beloved by so many women, and who was so far in debt as your Hernandez. Thus . . . is one of those miserable hide-wallopers so much as point hees finger at my guitar, I will shoot it off and wear it on my watch chain."

Pecos, still watching the camp, drawled in his easy Texas manner: "You haven't got a watch chain. You gambled it away in Miles."

"What good was the chain after I had given my watch to that *señorita* in Deadwood?"

"She stole it from you."

Big Jim awoke and said in a voice that was unexpectedly treble: "Gosh, Butch, I should think you'd save your money and see if you could pay back some of your debts."

"Lend me your tobacco and stop hounding me. Why should you be worrying about those few miserable thousand dollars I am owing you? Have I not said that the debts of Hernandez Pedro Gonzales y Fuente Jesús María Flanagan are sacred, and he will go on owing them, every last *centavo*, forever and ever?"

They rode on, down a long slope, through little badlands hills, and came out at the camp only a couple hundred yards away. The Indians were howling drunk, beating tom-toms. There was never a shortage of liquor at the Big Dry. It was a favorite route among whisky traders who wanted to avoid Army inspection at Fort Missouri or the Musselshell.

Rough, whiskered men, armed and suspicious, lounged around the wagons, watching their approach. They could get five years in federal prison for dealing in Indian whisky, and any man might be a government spy.

Pecos finally recognized one of them and called: "Hello, McLouse!"

His real name was McLauch, but he'd been called McLouse for so many years he'd almost forgotten. He was a stooped, powerful, filthy man with fierce red whiskers and a huge cheekful of tobacco. "Well, I'm damned if it ain't the fast gun from Texas. You still shooting the corks off from bottles at a hundred apiece?"

He was referring to the day two years ago when Pecos had won four hundred in a shooting contest with Captain Steele, a circus marksman, down in Laramie. Pecos made some remark about two-bit exhibition gunmen, got down with saddle stiffness crippling his legs, and asked: "What you got here, a renegade's convention?"

"Ferry cable broke. This is a hell of a place. Kid, you won't believe it, but the grub run out five days ago and nobody's even noticed."

"Those Indians haven't."

"Gros Ventre." He held the tribe in contempt. "Listen to 'em howl. Everybody drunk. Squaws and all. But they'll sober up directly. They're down to trading off their breechclouts."

Pecos let the bridle drag and walked over to a place of canvas and cribbed logs that proved to be a saloon. A tall man with a braying voice and a prominent Adam's apple was riding herd on the jug, arguing politics with his customers, siding with the U.P. in the Credit Mobilier scandal.

He stopped suddenly in the middle of a sentence when he saw Pecos with Hernandez and Big Jim behind him. "Say, you're the Pecos Kid!" he said, elbowing around the bar.

Pecos hid his surprise and said: "Why, yes, seh."

"I'm Missou. That's enough for me if the Pecos Kid's

enough name for you." He winked and dug down in his pocket. Then he changed his mind and looked back inside the tent at the men who were watching them. He said from the side of his mouth: "You come along. Got something for you. Been waiting to give it to you for three days."

Pecos laughed and said: "Why, I'd call that nothing short of remarkable, seeing we didn't even know we were comin' here until sunup this mawnin'."

"You're here, aren't you?" Missou had hold of his shirt sleeve, pulling him along.

"Seh, take your hands off me."

"All right. Don't get ringy. You come yonder."

He vaulted inside a covered wagon, and Pecos, stiff and tired, followed him.

A breathless heat lay beneath the wagon sheets. He waited as Missou drew from his pocket a letter bent and dirty from long carrying.

Pecos opened it. Two lines were scrawled with the blunt point of a bullet:

See Jawn Ridley at Citadel Rock. Come at night.
M.C.

He read it, let a laugh jerk his shoulder, wadded the paper, and thrust it in his Levi's. "Just like that! See Jawn Ridley! Now who gave this M.C. the idea he could tell me to see anybody?"

"That's Mike Coffey. He's foreman at Citadel Rock. He speaks for Jawn Ridley, all right, and, when Jawn tells a man to come, he *comes*." Missou bent over in the middle from laughter. "Either that, or he moves to that renegade town at Bull Sink."

"The hell with him."

Missou opened his eyes wide and said: "If you want my advice. . . ."

"I don't."

Pecos got down from the wagon. Big Jim and Hernandez were waiting. For just a moment he looked drawn and tired, older than his twenty-eight years.

Missou, still not able to believe that anyone would defy the command of Jawn Ridley, shouted after him: "Hey, you're going to Citadel, aren't you?"

"I said the hell with him. If Ridley wants to see me, let him go north to Milk River."

It was sundown. The Pecos Kid lay on his back with his hat over this eyes and an empty coffee cup on his chest.

Hernandez, after a third reading of the letter, said: "There is one thing to consider, and that is the matter of *pesos,* of which thees Jawn Ridley undoubtedly has plenty. Now. . . ."

"To hell with him."

Hernandez cried: "And to hell weeth you! First in one breath you tell me to pay off my debts, and in the next you snap your fingers at thees *Señor* Moneybags who owns half the cattle in Montana Territory. What is there about Milk River that you would go there?"

"I want to drown you in it." He sat up, putting aside his hat and coffee cup. There was a big fight in progress at the Gros Ventre camp, everyone screaming at once. Pecos listened without too much interest. He went on: "All right, I'll tell you. I served in the Army during the wah. In the Army, when your superior says *put your pants on backward and wade eight feet through green swamp,* you do it. So when I was mustered out and headed nawth. . . ."

"But what has thees to do with *pesos* for the pockets of Hernandez?"

"I had my bellyful of being ordered around. Anyhow, I got word on a silver strike. Pal up yonder on the Sweetgrass. Apperson, sergeant, Tully's Brigade. Maybe it'll be another Comstock."

In the morning, stripped, with clothes bundled on their saddles, they crossed the river, swimming, holding to the horses' tails. They followed the freight road north, spending the night at a squawman's shanty on the Little Bow, and mid-afternoon next day reached a town of cottonwood log shanties on a bench overlooking Milk River—the new northern terminus of the Texas cattle herds.

It had rained the night before, turning the single winding street into a quagmire. Half a hundred men were gathered near a freight outfit that had just made the long drag from Benton by way of the Bear Paws. All the talk concerned tobacco, of which, apparently, there was a shortage.

They tied up at a hitch rack, waded in their boot heels, and stamped sticky gumbo mud on the corduroy sidewalk.

Men drifted back from the freight wagon, still talking about tobacco. It was a rough town, with citizens to match—Indian traders in buckskins and moccasins, prospectors, trappers, and cowboys who for reasons of their own had chosen to ride farther than their companions, and pause within a night's travel of the Canadian border.

Across the street stood a long, log freight house, but aside from that the town was just a double line of keg and tincup saloons.

Pecos inquired all along the street before finding anyone who'd ever heard of Apperson. His mine, in the Sweetgrass country, proved to be a hundred miles west.

"Hell, that's nothing in this country." But the Pecos Kid looked discouraged. He needed a drink. One round of raw trade liquor took the last three dollars from his pocket.

At the trading post they learned that foodstuffs sold for a dollar a pound regardless of kind. It was evening then, and he led them inside a dim, greasy little restaurant.

"How much you got?" he asked Big Jim.

Jim cried defensively: "I scratched and saved and got ninety-five dollars sewed up inside . . . where I ain't telling . . . and I'm not letting it go. Damn it, I'm sick of being drug from one range to the other, a flat-busted saddle tramp."

He was still talking when a lanky old man in a flour sack apron came down behind the counter, served three cups of coffee, and said: "Beef steak, risin' bread, beans, rice, and dried apple pie. Five dollars buys you a ticket around the horn."

Pecos said: "We'll go around the horn. Jim, get that money unpinned from your drawers. You wouldn't let your friends starve for a sneakin' little fifteen dollars."

A man had come inside. He stopped with his back to the door, cutting off the evening light. Feeling his gaze, Pecos looked around. The man was large, angular, and powerful, about forty. Pecos had never seen him before. He was certain of that. He had the sort of face you'd remember.

"Pecos?" the man asked.

"Well, I'm damned. This is getting a bit ridiculous. Every place I stop. Yes, seh, I'm called Pecos."

The man smiled with a tightening of his lips and walked on, coming down hard in his mud-smeared riding boots. He still smelled of fresh horse, so he'd just dismounted after long riding. There were some coins in his big, red-freckled hand. Gold coins. "Fifteen?" He tossed out a ten and a five, and he still had a heavy weight of gold to rattle.

It was a friendly sound and with bright, smiling eyes Hernandez arose, swept off his hat, and bowed low. "*Señor,* would you do us the honor of coming to dine with us?"

Pecos said: "Sit down." Then to the stranger: "Thanks, but we got money."

"Of course. This is just *Northern* hospitality."

"What are you . . . the Milk River welcoming committee?"

"No, the other way around. I came to *get* you. You caused me one hell of a chase. All the way from Big Dry."

"You're Mike Coffey. You're the man who left the letter."

He nodded.

"Sorry, Coffey, but we just got here. We're not leaving town."

"I'd guess that you *were*."

Anger showed in the sudden narrowing of the Pecos Kid's eyes. He swung away from the counter. The movement seemed slack and casual, but it freed his holstered .45. Coffey kept smiling. His intensely blue eyes showed amusement.

"Did I say you gave *me* one hell of a chase? I should have said *us*. I'm not alone." He tilted his head toward the rear of the dim eating place.

Several men had moved quietly through the kitchen. A half-breed with short, ribbon-bound braids, stood ahead of the others with a sawed-off shotgun in the crook of his arm. There were other men out front.

Pecos sensed their presence without looking around. "Euchred," he said, with the old easy drag in his voice. "Yes, seh, you pulled the pack on me. I guess I should be flattered, only you got me overrated. One gun would be sufficient."

"I got nothing against you, Pecos. It's just that Jawn Ridley said *come,* and you didn't."

"They always come when Ridley says that?"

"'Most always." He plucked the Colts, first from Pecos's holster, then Big Jim's and Hernandez's. "Now go ahead and enjoy your supper. We'll wait out back. You hear that? . . . *out back.* I'd rather nobody saw us leaving town together."

"Is it too much to ask what in the devil Ridley wants? Why all this back door, dark of the moon . . . ?"

"That's something, I dare say, you'll find out a couple of nights from now when you talk to Jawn Ridley face to face."

II

"Big Jawn Ridley"

They rode for many miles with only small talk passing among them, camping about midnight at an abandoned trapper's shanty in a nameless coulée.

"I'll take that gun back now," Pecos said to big Mike Coffey.

"No. You boys had a hard trip through a bad country. You need some rest and relaxation. We'll do any shooting that needs being done, and you do the sleeping."

Pecos laughed and said: "Thank you, seh."

At dawn they were in the saddle again, riding southwestward across high prairie. Morning passed, and afternoon. Ahead lay the Missouri River badlands, sharply revealed in the yellow highlight and purple shadow of a late sun. Here and there they had a glimpse of the river, with the summits of Medicine Ridge rising beyond.

Coffey, riding beside Pecos, pointed with an outflung arm and said: "Yonder's The Citadel. 'Way across. That first terrace of the ridge, just short of the steep rocks. You can see the white shine the big house makes. I guess it's about all of twenty miles off."

"He calls it that . . . The Citadel?"

"It's a good name."

They stopped at a horse camp of the Stinchfield Cattle Company where without question a cowboy cut out fresh mounts for them. The trail now took them off the prairie rim, down long coulées, across cottonwood flats just above the river. There was a freight road and, shortly after sundown, a landing with a flatboat ferry where a small, weather-beaten man sat hunched over a book. He didn't glance up even when the horses *clomped* almost atop him and rocked the boat so its forward end dipped water.

Coffey said: "Hello, Good-Eye. You still reading that same book?"

He looked up then, and Pecos could see his right eye was a blind milky white.

The ferry creaked and strained against its wire cable as the power of the spring current propelled it across. It came to rest on a rather substantial log and plank steamboat dock with a counterbalanced landing stage to get the horses ashore without swimming. On a bench above high water stood a couple of cabins, and a warehouse bearing on its staff the emblem of the **St. Louis and Montana Trading Company**. It was still a five minute ride through cottonwoods before the rest of the little settlement came into sight.

"Medicine Landing?" inquired Pecos.

"*Ridley* Landing," Coffey said.

Pecos laughed. "Why, the country's sure enough changing. It used to belong to just the Injuns and God. Now I guess it's even out of the hands of God."

The Landing was very old, having been established in 1844 for the Gros Ventre trade. Later it found itself on the north-south freight road, and, now that the freight outfits favored the western route by way of Benton and the Sweetgrass, it had become little more than a private landing for the big Ridley and Stinchfield cattle outfits.

The buildings, all ten of them, were of bleached cottonwood logs, all of one story, and apparently all, except a couple, were saloons. Lamps burned here and there, making splashes of yellow in the late twilight. From one of them came the *plink-plink* of a piano, and on the air was an odor of the empty beer barrels that had been stacked outside.

The Landing was left behind. The freight road led up a stream called the Big Muddy. Rising to the east in a series of pine-studded ridges was the hill and mountain country called Medicine Ridge.

"*Ridley* Ridge?" Pecos asked.

"Medicine," Coffey said.

The freight road, after wandering the bottoms, forked with one branch pointing westward toward Fort Wells on the Musselshell, while the other climbed Medicine Ridge by a series of rocky pitches. They turned eastward, dropped over the first high summit, and there found Ridley's home ranch spread beneath them.

Even in a country of big outfits it was something to see. There were many acres of sheds and pole corrals, tree-shaded with a mountain stream here and there making a flash in the night light as it meandered through them. Sheds and bunk-houses, built along a wagon road, gave the appearance of a small town. The foreman's house of white-painted logs stood on a low bench up from the creek.

The big ranch house, as though it were, indeed, a citadel, sat with a removed magnificence a quarter mile up the valley on a perfectly flat terrace, fronted and backed by steep banks of dirt and stone. It was a three-story structure of sawed lumber, white-painted, with a porch that doubled its apparent size. There were bigger houses in the territory, perhaps, but a man would travel to Last Chance before seeing them. It was awe-inspiring, indeed.

Coffey said: "Don't say too much. I wouldn't want the men to know who I'm bringing."

He didn't explain. Riding ahead, he took them on a roundabout trail along the hillside, until he was able to cut straight down to the steep bank that fronted the grounds. A man on watch revealed himself with movement and a bit of gun shine. He talked with Coffey, dropped again out of sight, then Coffey returned, and they sat for a few minutes, waiting. At the big house a screen door opened, slapped shut. A man, straight and powerful in silhouette, stood with lamplight behind him.

"All right," Coffey said, "you can go up there now."

That the great man himself? Pecos wondered as he rode off. "Sure you can trust me?" he said aloud. "I might just make a break for the up country."

"That'd mean we'd have to go get you all over again."

Pecos found a bridle path and followed it in a big figure five through the trees and shrubbery of the grounds. It gave him a chance to see Ridley long before Ridley could see him.

The man was probably in his early forties, although he looked younger. His face was narrow, with prominent bones. It was a strong face with a good jaw. His hair, dark brown and very curly, was cut in a long feather-edge. He wore a mustache so closely cropped it was hard to see in the backlighting from the door. He watched Pecos ride to a stop and dismount with an appraising, slightly amused expression.

"Major Warren!" he said. "Good of you to come!"

"I came with a gun in my back as you well know, seh. And I guess you can forget about the *Major* part of it. All that's a long way behind."

There was no smile on Ridley's face now, and his spine was stiff as a rifle barrel. "I'll never forget the butchery of the South, and neither will you!"

"Sorry, seh." He dismounted and walked the last twenty steps. "No offense to you or the South, but I meant it about leaving the war behind. I headed into a new country to start

135

over again, just like you did. Only I guess I haven't accumulated so much."

Ridley was smiling again. "Only the notches on your gun?"

"I don't carve notches. And now, if you'll tell me why you sent your gunmen to hunt me down and drag me here . . . ?"

"Sorry, Major."

"Just the *Pecos Kid,* remember?"

"Sorry, Pecos." He came down from the step to shake hands with him. His manner showed it was quite a concession. It was a concession Ridley would not have made to the governor of the territory, nor to the President of the Republic, but he made it to Pecos who, like himself, had once been an officer in the Confederate Army. He stood, slightly taller and much broader, one hand on Pecos's shoulder, and gestured outward at the vast home ranch spread on the creek bottoms below. "Sometimes things look more substantial than they are. It's not easy for a *Rebel* officer to get ahead and hold his gains in a country where all the cards are stacked by the Yankees. That's why I brought you here. I heard what you did down in Mescalero, and in Corbus City before that. So, when a stage driver said you were headed toward Big Dry Crossing from Miles, I sent them to bring you."

With Ridley's heavy hand still on his shoulder they went inside. Pecos could smell perfume, and a piano was playing. It gave him the strange feeling of suddenly walking into another world. He stopped at the edge of a big, dim, luxuriously furnished room. A girl stood with her back to a square piano, looking at him intently but without emotion. He'd never seen her before, yet her face hit him with a shock like recognition.

She stood very straight with her shoulders back and her head up. She was dressed in a riding skirt, a blouse, and tiny, square-toed boots. Her hair was wind-blown and fell in careless masses across her shoulders. Her riding skirt was wrinkled to the shape of her body. Her eyes were wide-set, her nose small, her mouth rather broad. Taken by themselves, none of her features was good, but put together they gave her a striking beauty, a beauty with fire and color in it.

Someone was still caressing the keys of the piano. Jawn Ridley snapped—"Albert!"—and a young man came instantly to his feet.

He was twenty or twenty-one, and tall as Ridley, but still he gave the impression of being miniature and weak. Ridley introduced them. The girl was Letty Stinchfield, and the boy was his son. The girl didn't say a word, but the boy, ill at ease, mumbled a greeting.

Ridley waited and with a movement of impatience broke in: "Holy hell, is that one of the things you learned in Saint Louis? This isn't the opera. You shake hands with a man in this country." Then, without giving him a chance to do it, he said: "Take Letty and go outside. Cigar?" he asked, but saw Pecos was rolling a cigarette. He bit off the end of a long, slim panatela, and strode after his son. "Albert . . . remember this . . . no one is to know the major or his two companions are here."

When he came back, Pecos said: "Now what's the meaning of all that? What difference if the whole world knows I visited you here at The Citadel?"

"Because you're going to work for me, and it might easily jeopardize your life." Motioning for Pecos to follow, he walked with a stiff stride across the room leaving the odor of fine Havana smoke behind him. He entered an office, pulled down the shades, and closed the door. Then, seated behind a massive mahogany desk, he studied Pecos's face. "An adventurer! You're a fool. You could light some place, make a fortune. This whole new country, like a horn of plenty, is opened for the taking."

Pecos sat slouched in a chair and laughed. "Some of us were just born to be saddle tramps."

"Not a man who was under Johnston!"

"Oh, hell! Let's hear no more of that. My commission came pretty late. I reckon it came because all the real majors got killed."

"Well, what *are* you interested in?"

The question should have been an easy one, but it made the Pecos Kid stop and think. Finally he said: "We were in Milk River looking for Jim Apperson. He's got a silver mine on the Sweetgrass."

Ridley put down his cigar so hard it knocked the ash off. There was a quick, impatient power in every move he made. He said: "I own eleven gold and silver prospects back here in Medicine Ridge. I bought them and closed them down to prevent miners setting fire to my range. They're not worth operating, but for all that I wouldn't trade them for the best mine on the Sweetgrass." As he talked, he unlocked a desk drawer. He took out a leather bag, weighted by metal, tossed it over. It landed with a heavy jingle.

"Is that for me, seh?"

Ridley jerked his head *yes*. "I play for big stakes. You'll find that the men who work for me also play for big stakes."

Pecos pulled the drawstring, looked inside. The yellow glow of golden double eagles had a certain phosphorescence. "Must be a thousand dollars here."

"You're a good guesser. There's exactly a thousand dollars."

"And what do we do for it?"

"You've already *done* for it. That's your pay for coming down from Milk River."

Pecos tossed the bag from one hand to the other. It was heavy—heavier than bullet lead, almost four pounds in a

138

cluster of gold pieces smaller than his fist. "Seh, this is very nice stuff, and in the past I've had considerable trouble resisting it. By the way, I think I *will* have one of those Havanas."

III

"Letty Stinchfield"

Two hours had passed, and the Pecos Kid stood outside alone, under a flawless night sky. A cool wind flowed up from the south, carrying the odor of sage and poplar, of spring growth and the river. He stood for a while at the edge of the porch. Someone moved, and he turned, thinking of the girl, Letty Stinchfield.

It was a man, lounging at ease against a pillar. He could tell nothing about him, except that he was slim and armed with two guns. Moonlight raised points of metallic shine from some silver conchos on his belt, from the crossed rows of cartridges, and from the guns that rode low on his thighs. Very low. Too low for a riding man. Ridley's bodyguard.

He must have known that Pecos saw him, but no word was spoken. Pecos went on down the steps and across the grounds, among dressed-down specimen shrubs, along some white crushed rock that had been laid between brick forms to make a carriage path.

Below, about a quarter mile away, he could see lights in the foreman's house. He'd find Hernandez and Jim there, but he was in no hurry. In the cool shadow of the grounds he took time to think about Jawn Ridley.

Ridley was right. It was hell for a man who'd been an officer on the Southern side when he went up against Northern law. Yonder, to the south, lay Horn Creek, the Big and Little Sage, and Bull Creek, forming, together with Medicine

Ridge, the heart of his cattle empire. And now, with the help of the Grand Army of the Republic in Helena, homesteaders were grabbing the best of it, fencing the springs, plowing under the deep buffalo grass that grew in the bottoms.

On hearing Ridley that far, the Pecos Kid had said: "You're not getting me to run any hoeman off your grass. The grass was free for you. It's free for them."

"My cattle and horses aren't free!"

And Ridley had gone on with his story, claiming that even with G.A.R. financial help, no rancher could make a living along those badlands streams without winter range in the Medicine Ridge. They weren't sodbusters. They were rustlers, living safely under the protection of the G.A.R., making a gesture at oat fields and spuds, but actually supplying rustled stock to the outlaw town of Bull Sink.

Pecos said: "I don't guess the G.A.R. would object too much if you rode down yonder with forty, fifty men and shot out a rustler town. With that gone. . . ."

"We tried that, three times. They were warned each time. Yes, I know what you're thinking . . . that they have men planted right here at my home ranch. That's why I kept your arrival as quiet as possible."

Ridley, with his violent manner, had come to a stop with his hands spread wide on the table. "That's why I need *you*. You have a reputation. Some people think you have a bad reputation. They'll accept you down in Bull Sink. Jack Kansas, Legless Joe Hames, and all the rest. This so-called Horn Creek Land Owners Association will accept you, too. I want you to go down there and take up a homestead."

"*Me?*"

"Yes. From now on you're a Union veteran. Here's the papers to prove it."

"Well, I'm damned. You think of everything."

141

That's how it had been. He'd agreed to take up the land, to do a business in rustled cows, and gather the information that would permit them to clean out the rustler's town of Bull Sink.

A sound from the shadows made him spin around, his hand by habit on his hip where the gun should have been. It gave him a peculiar, lost feeling to be without that three pounds of metal that had stood beside him through all the miles and years that separated him from the Pecos.

He first thought was of the gunman lounging on Ridley's porch. Then a perfume touched his nostrils. Very faint, but it hit him with a jolt of recognition. It was the girl. She was a silhouette now, moving through a vine-covered arbor. Her riding skirt, her shirt, and her skin were all dark, as though turned the same hue by the Western sun, and he had a hard time seeing her even when she was so close he could hear the slide of her smooth skin beneath the blouse.

Albert Ridley wasn't with her. She was alone. She knew whom he was looking for and laughed. "Albert? Why, he's afraid of me."

Pecos didn't ask why. He knew why. She was too much woman for him. Pecos walked toward her. She'd stopped at the edge of the shadows to wait for him. Her arms were at her sides, her head was back. She was smiling with lips pressed tightly together. It could have been contempt, or a challenge.

"You're one of the Stinchfields." Pecos meant one of *the* Stinchfields of the big Stinchfield Cattle Company across the river.

She nodded, and kept watching him. "I've heard of you, too. He introduced you as Major Warren. You're not *Major Warren*. You're the Pecos Kid. You're a gunman. I heard you were the fastest gunman who ever came north of Wyoming."

"They speeded me up a little."

"You're the man who killed Manuel Querno. You killed Star Glynn. You killed Sundance Billy."

"No, ma'am. You're thinking of somebody else. I didn't kill all those men." He laughed, and added: "Why, look at me. I don't even carry a gun."

"He brought you here to kill more men, didn't he?"

"You're jumping to conclusions."

"He brought you here to kill Jack Kansas."

Kansas was the one-time train robber who was now the rustler chief at Bull Sink. Pecos kept watching her eyes, wondering why she'd followed him.

"I take it Kansas is no friend of the Stinchfields. Why should it make any difference whether I came to the country to kill him or not?"

There was challenge in the tilt of her head and in her voice. "Maybe it'd be the other way around."

"Maybe. But Kansas ain't here. He's yonder sixty, seventy miles in Bull Sink. What are we doing talking about Kansas?" Pecos wondered.

She moved back from him, and he followed her deeper into the shadows. He had the strong impression that she wanted him to follow her. It was so dark he could see the oval of her face only vaguely.

She said: "When are the rest of them coming?"

"The rest of whom?"

"The gunmen you're bringing in from Miles?"

"I guess you'll have to see Ridley about that. I know nothing about gunmen from Miles."

"You're lying to me!"

"You're a beautiful woman. Beautiful women get lied to all the time, but not about things like that. I've come all the way nawth from Denver City without seeing a more beautiful woman than you."

143

She hitched one shoulder away and said: "Who was in Denver City?"

"You see, you're like all the rest. You can't endure hearing another woman is beautiful even at a thousand miles."

"What do I care who you took up with in Denver?"

It gave him an unsteady feeling, being so close to her. It was as though he'd had ten drinks of Ridley's brandy instead of only one. She started to move away again, and he seized her by the arms, just below her shoulders. She twisted back and forth with a quick, feline strength, but he held her.

She spat: "I'll call for help, and they'll kill you!"

"Who? Albert Ridley?"

"No!"

"That was a love song he was playing on the piano. You been around Albert too long. I don't play my love songs on the piano."

"Let me go!" She didn't want him to let her go.

He said: "You shouldn't have followed me."

"I didn't follow you."

"You're here."

"I didn't want you to get killed."

"At Bull Sink?"

"He *is* sending you over there, then!" She waited for him to answer, but his mind was a long way from Bull Sink. She said: "Why did you come here after dark by the hill trail, on the quiet? Why are your friends down there in Mike Coffey's house with newspapers pinned over the windows? Why'd he introduce you as *Major* Warren? You're just a hired gunman! Usually he wouldn't allow a hired gunman inside the house."

"You still worrying about whether I'll get killed?"

Now she really tried to get away. "No! I don't care what happens to you. Quit it. You're hurting my arm!" She bent over, twisting halfway around, and slipped out of his grasp.

She backed into the arbor. Vines had grown up the sides, but there was a rift across the roof where the moon shone through. "Stop!" she whispered.

He did. The moon reflected cold blue from the double Derringer in her hand. He laughed and managed to make it sound natural. "What's all this talk about you calling for help? You're one woman that don't need to call for help."

She spoke behind her little, white teeth. "What did he say when you were inside the office?"

"I forgot. I think he said you were the most beautiful woman this side of Denver. And I told him he was wrong. I told him there was nobody in Denver that could even compare with you."

As he talked, his eyes roved the arbor. A hammock had been stretched at one side. There was a seat heaped with sofa pillows along the other. His hands, hanging at his sides, were just above the bench. With a natural swing of his right hand he took one of the pillows, lifted it, and, before she realized what had happened, it was in front of the Derringer. She tried to get the gun free, but he followed, the pillow at arm's length, pressed against the muzzle.

He said: "There's nothing like a pillow to stop bullet lead. Why, this pillow would slow up a Forty-Five. That little cap and ball wouldn't stand a chance."

She said something through her teeth. She twisted and bent over. It was like a fencing contest. The gun exploded. He felt the shock of it, and it almost tore the pillow from his fingers. The bullet plowed through and struck him without piercing his clothes. He struck her wrist a chopping blow and knocked the gun to the ground, its second barrel still unexploded. She dived for it, but he was ahead of her.

"A Forty-Five," he said. "Why, that's an important caliber."

He pulled the cap out and tossed the gun aside. There was nothing to stop her from getting away, but she didn't.

He seized her by the arms again. He drew her hard against him. She didn't resist. She neither clung to him nor fought him. She was perfectly pliable in his arms. He had the feeling that she would have fallen if he hadn't been there to support her. He kissed her. Her lips made no response. They were slightly open. Her eyes were open, staring at him.

A man was running along one of the gravel paths. It was Albert Ridley. He stopped about twelve strides away. The breeze carried an odor of gunsmoke, and he couldn't help locating it. They were revealed by the moonlight shining through the rift in the vines. He turned away, pretending not to have seen them.

"Al, where are you, Al?" a man called in a nasal voice. He came at a wobbly half run, having trouble with his riding boots. Conchos gleamed on his belt, the butts of silver-mounted revolvers gleaming against his thighs. It was that gunman who'd been posted on the porch. He stopped and said: "Oh, there you are. What was that shot?"

"I guess it was down at the bunkhouse," Al replied.

After the two men left, walking back to the ranch house, Pecos and Letty came out of the shadows. The girl took a deep breath and moved suddenly, pulling herself away.

"I have to go!"

He didn't try to stop her. She remembered the gun, came back, looked around for it, found it, snatched it up, and tucked it inside the waist of her riding skirt. Then she really was gone, and for a long time he stood looking into the darkness that had swallowed her.

IV

"Bull Sink"

Their homestead was on Horn Creek, twenty-eight miles east of Medicine Ridge, a relinquishment purchased from a father and two sons who'd left the year before to do horse and scraper work for the Northern Pacific. The only buildings were a shack of cottonwood logs and a horse shed. A rail fence still circled the garden spot, bright green from volunteer spuds. Another fence that had been built around a spring had been pushed down, and, when they had first ridden up, half a dozen steers wearing the Ridley brand were inside, bedded down on the cool, damp earth.

They put the shack in order and immediately went to work on some of Ridley's cattle, using a running iron to alter his Rocking R to a Circle B. On the third day of this, Pecos, who was standing look-out on some cutbank rims, signaled down to the branding fire that visitors were coming.

There were three men—the Rutledge brothers from the upper reaches of the Big Sage, and rugged old Gus Hyslop from a few miles down on Horn Creek. Harry Rutledge, a tall, bent-over man of thirty-five, jogged up bareback on a muley broncho. His legs dangled so far his toes almost touched the ground. He wore bib overalls that looked too big for him because of the gun cinched around his waist. After introducing himself, his brother Fred, and Hyslop, he squinted all around. "I heered you'd took up Parker's relinquishment. This'd be a fair place for spuds, if a man would dam that

147

coulée to irrigate from the spring run-off, but it'd take five miles of contour ditching to bring the crick around." He wasn't thinking about spuds. He was trying to see how the boys had been spending their time. "There's a good market for spuds at Benton, if you could get 'em there. Too bad Benton ain't downstream so you could float your garden truck on the current. Laws, how they pay for it at the gold camps!"

"Why don't you ship by steamboat?"

He cackled out a laugh. "Try getting 'em to take anything aboard. Ridley owns a third interest in the Saint Louis and Montana, and he's got the power to tell Baker and the rest of 'em to head in, too." He kept looking around. "What you planted?"

"Nothing yet." Pecos had dismounted. He stood now with one elbow on the saddle, his manner saying that he was a cowboy, and no cowboy worth his keep would stoop to planting spuds or taking milk away from a calf.

Old Hyslop growled: "Ever have experience plantin' anything?"

Pecos narrowed his eyes and said: "Yeah, I planted a couple o' things along my way. I planted 'em six feet deep. Why'd you ask?"

Hyslop moved, cleared his throat, and kept his hands very wide of the old double-barreled shot pistol he had in his saddle holster. He was trying to keep watch of Jim Swing at the coulée narrows, of Hernandez who was just riding up through the sage-colored bullberry bushes, and of Pecos, all at the same time.

Fred Rutledge asked: "How you expect to make the place pay?"

"Few cows. Forty or fifty. We got a brand registered. Circle B. We'll manage."

"You'll have a fight on your hands if you start running stock toward the Medicine Ridge," Fred Rutledge said, "and that's the only place you'll find winter range. Every Jan'wary this prairie Chinooks and freezes over so even a stud horse with chalk shoes couldn't dig down to grass."

Hyslop, peering back through the narrows, asked: "Those your critters yonder?"

"Yes."

"Must have been just branding. We got a whiff of burning hair from 'way yonder, over the ridge."

Hernandez rode the last few yards in time to overhear him. He reined in and turned in the saddle so the butt of his six-gun was away from his body, ready to grab. "*Señor*, you perhaps accuse us of running the brand?"

"I ain't accusing nobody of nothing. But I do say this . . . *we* been accused of rustling, and we don't like it. I 'low we have to trade at Bull Sink, and I 'low that's a rustler's town, but we do it because we have to. We do it because the wildcat steamboats put in at Bull Landing, and they're the only ones that'll take our stuff aboard. It'd tickle Jawn Ridley pink if he could catch some of us homesteaders with brand-run cattle. Then he could go to the G.A.R. and say . . . 'Look who you been makin' loans to, a bunch of rustlers.' Well, it ain't going to happen. I'm not sayin' you *are* rustlers. All I'm saying is that we won't tolerate rustlin' by airy one of the homesteaders, you or anybody else."

It left him red-faced and out of breath. It took some guts to face them, scared as he was. He chewed savagely on his tobacco and spat.

Hernandez, playing his part, seemed ready to make trouble, but Pecos said—"Wait!"—and placed himself between them. "You got nothing to worry about, Hyslop. If you think we been running brands, tell you what we'll do . . . we'll let Ridley or his foreman or anybody else examine 'em."

They stayed for an hour, talking about other things, and rode away.

"I theenk I saw doubt in their eyes," Hernandez said.

"That's how I wanted it. They'll talk, and the word that we're running Ridley's brand will get around. In a week it'll get to Bull Sink. Then we'll drive our critters down and see what sort of price Kansas will pay."

They started through the June twilight, and kept the fifty cattle at an alternate trot and walk over the broad bulge of prairie that separated the Horn from Bull Creek. Following Bull Creek, they entered the badlands, a maze of barren, steep-sided buttes separated by dry cañons, a country of gray clay, whitish sandrock, with here and there a seam of lignite that was weathered rusty red from its iron content. Some of the cañon walls were vertical, four or five hundred feet high, with sandrock pillars towering above them still higher, and by night they seemed massive, like the Rockies.

There was a fair trail down the Bull, with a trickle of water appearing and disappearing in the gravel. Along past midnight the coulée walls fell away, and they reached a hundred-acre stretch of fairly level bottom where groves of cottonwoods and box elders made billowing black and silver masses by moonlight.

No one had spoken for an hour. They'd been wary, thinking about a bullet from some rustler's gun. Pecos stopped while the cattle waded knee-deep through the muck of a spring hole, and Big Jim rode up beside him.

Jim said: "We must be close to that outlaw town."

Even after all the months and miles they'd drifted together, it was sometimes a surprise to hear the treble quality of the big fellow's voice.

"It's yonder, I guess. Four or five miles."

"They'd sure as hell have a look-out."

"Unless Jack Kansas feels strong enough to outgun the whole country."

"Maybe he *can* outgun the whole country!"

"Now, there's a thought. Maybe he can. Maybe it's like Jackson Hole. They do a lot of talking about shooting the rustlers out of The Hole, too, but I don't notice 'em doing it."

"You ever been in Jackson, Kid?" Jim said.

"That's a damned dirty insult, but in point of fact it just happens that I was." He laughed about it and added: "Old fellow named Holzheimer and me was prospecting the headwaters of Wind River when a war party of Crows raided our camp and left us without so much as a horse, a biscuit, or a blanket. We had our choice of walking all the way down to Green River on the U.P. or dropping across to The Hole, so to The Hole we went. Rustlers, robbers, Army deserters, why, they were thick as Baptists in Missouri. Horse rustlers mainly. Must have been two thousand head of horses on those big hay bottoms and not one of 'em honestly owned. Town there. Saloons, gamblin' houses, girls . . . they *called* 'em girls. Sweet name o' hell! The looks of some of those girls would have turned the stomach of a man that'd been skinnin' buffalo in hot weather."

"Tough town?"

"Tough! It'd make Miles City look like Pea Patch, Iowa on Sunday mawnin'. You raid a man's cache in that town and the penalty is hanging quick as they can get a rope over a tree, but kill him in a gunfight and it wouldn't even make a subject for conversation."

"You think Bull Sink's like that?"

"I'd imagine, seeing the same talent created both of 'em. I'll wager that some of the men you'll find in Bull Sink were two weeks ago in Jackson Hole, and two weeks from now will be back there. Horse rustlin' . . . there's the business for a man that wants to get around. It's no accident you find so many Dakota horses down in Colorado."

They took turns sleeping and watching. At sunup the cattle were already scattered, grazing the buffalo grass that grew among the sage.

Pecos said: "They'll stay here for a couple days. We'll drift on to Bull Sink. It can't be more'n six or eight miles."

The coulée narrowed and widened again. Other coulées, equally as large, came in from east and west. The walls were no longer continuous. Here it was a country of round-topped buttes with steep sides, each one like the other so it was almost impossible to pick out a landmark anywhere.

"Gun shine," Big Jim said. He said the word without turning.

The other two stiffened a little, but didn't look around. They kept going at the same pace.

"Where?" Pecos asked.

"Almost into the sun, by that sandrock strip about a hundred yards up."

"We must have ridden right by him."

"He had a good shot. He's still got a good shot, if he wants it."

Finally, with three hundred yards between them, Big Jim took his hat off and mopped sweat off his broad cheeks. "Don't that give you an itch between the shoulder blades?"

Hernandez said: "Ha! What is there to fear? Have I not already told you how the Gypsy said I would die reech and respected, in bed, with my boots off, and all my debts paid up?"

"They never told *me* any of those things?" Big Jim responded.

Here the ground showed signs of considerable travel. A large cañon came in from the east, its floor trodden to dust by the hoofs of horses. A dugout shanty against one of the cañon walls overlooked several acres of horse corrals. Another turn in the coulée brought the town of Bull Sink into view.

It stood in a basin where at some prehistoric time the Missouri had gouged out a huge valley. On two sides, about a mile apart, rose steep bluffs. The ancient channel ran unobstructed to the east, but hillocks of glacial drift made a barrier in its other direction, and the present course of the river was about three and a half miles away. The glacial drift, that evidently had turned the river, had also dammed Bull Creek and formed a shallow lake or sink. It was almost perfectly circular, a quarter mile in diameter, ringed by soda-white alkali. The shanty buildings of the town were scattered over a low, glacial hillock beyond.

The town was larger than any of them had expected. Most of the shanties had slanting, dirt-covered roofs on which wild sweet peas had taken root, making bright yellow splashes of color. Gros Ventres lived in wickiups and skin lodges that had attained a depth of filth that spoke of permanence. Counting lodges and all, there were at least thirty-five dwellings. On the highest ground, forming a short street, were some false-fronted buildings. A couple of them were built of sawed lumber that of necessity had been freighted up the river.

The largest building, a weather-gray, ramshackle of two stories, bore remnants of a sign reading: **The Red Flag Dance Hall**.

Hernandez exhaled, kissed his fingertips, and said: "Ha, a pitfall! Filled with women! Are you not glad that I brought my guitar along? Tonight I serenade these beautiful creatures of Bull Sink weeth the love songs of all Sonora!"

153

"Listen, Butch, we came here on business," Pecos reminded.

"You choose your business and I'll choose mine. I am supposed to act like a cattle rustler, eh? A *bandido*. In my country, when a *bandido* comes to town, his heart cries out to love."

"You get into any trouble over one of these bedraggled dance-hall skirts, and you'll damned well get out of it by yourself."

But Hernandez, his eyes closed, was strumming his guitar and singing.

¡Ay, ay, ay, ay!
Canta y no llores. . . .

A few Indians watched them. Not a saddle horse was tied along the main street. Three men, all beyond middle years, sat on a strip of platform walk in front of a dingy log saloon bearing the sign **Dinny's Chicago Bar**.

Pecos drew up, got one leg crooked around the horn, and felt for his tobacco. "Where's everybody?"

The eldest, most bewhiskered, and filthiest of the three got his chaw of tobacco off to one side, and took his time about answering. "If you'd been here about eight hour ago, you wouldn't need to ask. Wasn't a man in five miles not at the flat watching Honeyjo Lee and that new gal of Robin's battle it out. Why is it when two women get in a ruckus, they tear each other's clothes off?" He giggled. "Never saw two women do so much clothes-rippin' with so little to start with."

Hernandez alighted and said: "Where are they now?"

"Oh, you're away too late."

They talked about other things, and finally Pecos brought up the name of Jack Kansas.

"He sleeps yonder, upstairs in the Flag. That's his joint. Partners with Legless Joe Hames. But you won't see him before afternoon. What have you boys got . . . some Wyomin' horses?"

"Cattle. Local stock."

"Well, I dunno. I came down here once with eight head of Two Dot mavericks, and all I got for 'em was six dollars each. Kansas might give you tobacco money for 'em, but cows are a little out of his line."

Pecos got down and jingled his spurs around the hitch rack. The street was deeply trodden, its dust filled with glass, shot-out cartridges, and withered playing cards. He said: "Those nesters yonder on the bench aren't *horse* rustlers."

"They're nothing if you want my estimate. They'll end by getting Jawn Ridley down on us."

Pecos didn't ask too many questions. He loafed around town, making acquaintances, listening, watching. Bull Sink was lawless but easy-going, filled with saddle bums, Army deserters, and longriders. Nobody worked, and yet there was plenty of money around.

About mid-afternoon a big, stiff-backed man with powerful legs came across from the Red Flag, gave Pecos a long, narrow scrutiny, and said: "I hear you got some cows you're thinking of selling to Jack Kansas."

Pecos got lazily to his feet and answered: "I'm open to a dicker."

Big Jim got up, too, and Hernandez came to the saloon door behind them.

"You tell your friends to stay here," the big man said, and led him across the street. As they walked, he repeated Pecos's name a couple of times. "Pecos. The Pecos Kid. Are you the Pecos Kid that was neck-deep in the bloody Clayton?"

"I was there."

"Corbus City? Mescalero?"

"Yeah."

He laughed. "Say, you been from place to place. You hunt those ruckuses out, or do you start 'em?"

"I didn't start 'em. I'm as peaceful as a jack rabbit at a rattlesnake's reunion."

"This your idea of a peaceful town?" He sounded a laugh in his bull throat. "Maybe it's your idea of a rattlesnake's reunion! You wouldn't've thought it was peaceful last night. Couple of gals got to fighting over the boss and tore off everything except the skin they were born in."

They walked from sunshine to the shadow and foul air of the Red Flag, through a short hall, up some stairs. Bullets had carved rough furrows on both of the walls, but it had been long ago, and now they'd collected cobwebs and dust.

"Don't say anything to the boss. He has a hanker for one of 'em."

"Honeyjo Lee?"

"Yeah, that's her. She's blastin' powder on a short fuse, that yella gal." As they walked along a dusty upper hall, the man got around to introducing himself as Hoss McFadden. He stopped at a door, then rapped, then shouted—"Jack? Here he is."—and, without waiting for an answer, moved inside.

It was a big room dominated by a circular poker table. Chairs, bottles, and glasses were everywhere. It smelled gassy from a kerosene lamp. The lamp had been burning unnoticed since the night before, its wick deep in a glass bowl, absorbing the last drops of oil.

Hoss McFadden blew out the lamp, saying: "This place smells like a cellar after the skunks moved out. Jack, you hear me? This is the Pecos Kid."

Jack Kansas had been asleep on a leather couch. He sat up,

rubbed fingers through his curly hair, and spat. He looked at Pecos as though the sight hurt his eyes, and stood up. He carried his gun gambler-style, high on his waist, so, when he was seated, his chair wouldn't get in the way. He'd been asleep with it on. His clothes were of good quality, but wrinkled. He was about Pecos's age, but twenty pounds heavier. He was round-faced and handsome in the manner that sporting men are often handsome. He wasn't built like a cowboy, but he'd ridden a lot, one could see that in his hip-shot manner as he stood.

He picked up a bottle. It was empty. The next one was also empty. He hoisted other bottles, all empty. He cursed, threw one of them, drew his gun in the same movement, and blasted it into jagged fragments as it hit the floor. He threw another, blasting it, and then another. The room was filled with gun stench and the ringing aftermath of concussion. Outside, men looked up at the room without stirring from their loafing places.

The shooting made Jack Kansas feel better. He grinned and said: "That's what I should have done to those bottles when they were full last night."

A rugged, glowering, black-whiskered man hobbled in, using a long-barreled Sharps rifle for a crutch. He was carrying a bottle of Old Haversill bourbon that he put down on the table. Looking at Pecos, he said: "I hear you're holding fifty head of cattle at Squawblanket Springs. Circle B. Just two strokes of a running iron away from a Rocking R. A good brand to get hung with."

Pecos laughed and said: "Rope-shy?"

"Yes, I'm rope-shy. You would've, too, if you'd had two brothers hung in front of your eyes, and hanging is what'll happen to some of us if we tangle with that big lobo, Jawn Ridley. I say we're better off sticking with horses."

Kansas laughed, and winked, and said: "This is my pard, Legless Joe Hames. He used to be a real ring-tailed ripper. He'd go right up and spit in the cougar's eye."

"I'll still spit in the cougar's eye, but not in Ridley's. You take my advice, you'll send this Pecos Kid out of here with his brand-run cattle and to hell with him."

"That wouldn't be cordial. I guess we'll buy those cows. How about five dollars a head? Five times fifty runs to around quarter of a thousand."

Pecos said: "You'll not buy 'em for five dollars a head."

"No? Well, that's up to you." He smiled a little and looked at Pecos with narrowed appraisal. "What you plan to do with 'em? Take 'em back across Ridley's range? Otherwise, I'll have to charge you a small fee for protection. Say . . . five dollars a head. Add it up this way, Kid . . . five you don't have to pay, plus five I'll pay you, amounts to ten dollars a head."

Legless Joe said: "I'd take those critters and not pay him so much as a Confederate dollar. Bringing 'em down here, getting Ridley on our necks. . . ."

"Keep quiet and pour the man a drink."

Pecos cursed, downed the liquor, and cursed some more. "All right. You got me. Let's see the two-fifty."

Jack Kansas paid him off in gold pieces, flipping them one after another in the air, watching them jingle to rest on the poker table. At two-fifty he laughed and flipped out another double eagle.

"There. That's for a couple of drinks. Sometime maybe we'll get together and cook up a *real* deal."

V

"A Real Hellcat"

At sundown, eight weather-beaten riders hit town driving nearly a hundred head of horses, mixed saddle and work stock, all sweat-streaked and dusty from hard travel. With the horses inside a field west of town, the men had a meeting with Jack Kansas from which they clumped giving out the aroma of freshly consumed whisky, their pockets a-jingle with gold pieces.

Sitting at a card table, listening to their talk, Pecos learned that the horses had come from the Dakota-Minnesota border, that they would be held in Bull Sink to be swapped for a herd expected up from Wyoming—and if the Wyoming stock didn't show, for stock from Washington, Idaho, or Canada. Such horses, with brands of distant registry, would be driven back by the Dakota rustlers, and disposed of openly at the horse auctions in Bismarck and Grand Forks, while Jack Kansas, for his clearing-house operation, would net a profit of each sixth animal that went through his hands.

The influx of horses and money brought the languishing town to life. A grotesquely fat woman known by the name of Wattles appeared and started hammering a piano while her undersize husband squeaked on a fiddle. Three dance-hall girls with tired, kalsomined faces were in constant demand as partners at four bits a dance.

The Pecos Kid walked out when Wattles commenced to sing in a bleak, shrill soprano:

Oh pity, oh pity the poor drunkard's child,
A poor little waif, six years old,
Barefoot and in rags she wandered
O'er cobblestones dreary and cold.

Pecos stayed at the Chicago Bar, playing solitaire with a greasy old deck. He played game after game. Everyone was at the Red Flag. Finally Big Jim burst in.

"Kid, you come with me. We got to get him out o' there, or he'll get drilled. You know what he's done? He's. . . ."

"Sure, I know. The same thing he did at Mescalero, Tres Castillos, and Lordsburg . . . the same as in Dodge and Coffee Creek and Cheyenne. He's after somebody's woman, but he's not buried in any o' those towns."

"He wasn't after Jack Kansas's woman in those towns!"

Pecos carefully laid a black trey on a red four. "I'd be moved to wager that Hernandez could draw and shoot and have time to spit before Kansas had his gun out of the leather." He could see Big Jim's underlip trembling, so he cursed, threw down the cards, and got to his feet. "All right, we'll go over there."

The Red Flag's lower floor was divided in two rooms by a colonnade of spindly pillars that had apparently been salvaged from a wrecked steamboat. Years of tobacco and lamp smoke had turned the interior a heavy brown. The bar was almost empty, with everybody pressed inside the dance hall where Wattles, her face like an enlarged tomato, was singing:

When the po-lice come to take you,
And your newfound friends forsake you
Remember your old mother deah
At ho-o-me, sweet home!

160

Pecos couldn't stand to look at her. He moved through, saying: "If there's one thing I can't endure, it's a drunken woman." He looked around. "Well, where is this Honeyjo?"

"He had her yonder . . . in that box."

There were four boxes at one side of the dance hall, their fronts covered with painted Chinese screens so their occupants could view the show without themselves being seen. There were no entrances from the dance-hall side, but Big Jim knew the way and took him down a short hall, past three doors to a fourth which was slightly ajar. Pecos looked inside. The box, a tiny cubicle, was filled with the odor of cigar, brandy, and a woman's perfume, but no one was there.

Outside, a shout had gone up, drowning out Wattles's song. She tried to shrill over it, then she gave up and retreated to the piano, where she commenced hammering a Negro steamboater's chantey, "The Yellow Gal of Natchez." It was still a few seconds before Pecos, looking through the dusty, painted screen, saw the cause of the outburst.

A girl had come out on the tiny stage. She was dark, slim in the waist, with full hips and bosom. She was not dressed like one of those bedraggled dance-hall girls. She wore a dress of amber satin that brushed the floor. It was a simple dress without ruffles or folderol. It might have been merely a strip of silk wrapped around her body with a tuck here, and one there, letting her own lines do the rest.

Her skin under the oil lamps had a tawny cast. She reminded Pecos of some jungle cat, ready to rub and purr at one second, or claw you to pieces the next. She smiled. Her teeth against her red-dyed lips and her dark skin seemed very white. As white as bits of shell. Her eyeballs had a white shine, too. She had black blood. She was a quadroon or an octoroon. Once, in New Orleans during the war, he'd been at a quadroon's ball and had seen a girl, who was almost her

counterpart, paying her favors from one young Creole to another, waiting with sulky indifference for the trouble to start.

He whistled softy and said: "That her? That Honeyjo
Lee?"

"Yes, that's her, and there's nothing she'd rather do than
get two men to killing each other."

"I don't wonder she had an audience when that clothes-
rippin' started last night."

Pecos wanted a better look at her. He managed to slide
one segment of the screen. She heard the sound and looked at
him. She looked and kept looking. She sang with a half smile,
swinging her hips in time with the music. She passed among
the tables, and one of the men made a grab for her, but with a
clever, sinuous movement she got out of his grasp.

Jack Kansas was seated in the look-out's chair above the
faro spread. She passed close to him, ignoring him, her eyes
on the Pecos Kid.

Pecos said to Jim from the side of his mouth: "I'm the one
you should be dragging out."

"*You* don't go clean loco over women."

"I might over this one."

She finished her song and walked out of sight through the
barroom. A little later she appeared in the doorway, smiled at
Pecos, and said: "I drink brandy. Portuguese brandy. They
got it. Especially fo' me, they got it. I'm letting you buy it fo'
me tonight."

Jim cried: "Pecos, listen here . . . !"

"Too late, Jim. You made a noble try, but I got no more
strength of resistance than Hernandez. On your way out, tell
'em to send the Portuguese brandy."

She watched Big Jim back out, watched the door swing
partly closed. Outside they were whooping it up and throwing
silver money around, wanting more verses of "The Yellow

Gal of Natchez," but she paid no attention. She reached a hand, very soft and strong and brown, got hold of Pecos's arm, and pulled him to the chair beside her.

The screen was still open. He suddenly realized that they were visible to Jack Kansas who still occupied the look-out chair. Kansas had cigarette between his lips. He spat it out, and stood, hitching up both his tight-fitting pants and his gun belt.

Pecos didn't try to get out of sight. He said: "You'd like to get me killed, wouldn't you?"

"Yo' scared o' *him?* I didn't think you'd be scared o' any man. Not the Pecos Kid. Not the man that outdrew Star Glynn."

She laughed, showing her strong white teeth. Now, seen closely, she wasn't so dark. Her skin was no darker than a south European's.

Jack Kansas was no longer in sight, but other men were watching. Legless Joe Hames stood against the far wall, propped on the Sharps rifle.

Pecos waved at Hoss, grinned, and slid the screen shut. Her arm was round his neck. She sat in his lap. She took his head in both hands and pulled it hard against her bosom. "I think you're the man for me, all right."

"But are you the woman for me?"

"I'm *plenty* o' woman." Smiling, she drew a little, slim-bladed dagger. "I should slit your throat. After I kiss yo', I'll slit your throat."

She stabbed the dagger in the table and kissed him. He wondered which would be worse, to have Kansas come through the door, or Hernandez. She leaned back. Her hair, in jet ringlets, hung toward the floor. Her eyes were closed, waiting for him to kiss her.

He said: "You wouldn't want a man to get shot over you!"

He called her a name, and said—"No, you wouldn't!"—and he kissed her.

Suddenly the door was booted open, and Kansas was there.

Instantly she was on her feet, between them. She faced Kansas. Her lips were drawn thin with contempt. She was ready to spit at him. Her voice was pitched so it could be heard in every part of the building: "Get out! Get out before Pecos kills you. He said you were a yellow horse thief. He said he'd kill you if you followed me."

He thought Kansas was going for his gun. He turned to get free of the table. His own gun was in his hand, but Kansas was trying to tear himself away from the girl. She'd sprung forward and was holding his right forearm with both hands. He hurled her away. The chair was behind her. The backs of her thighs hit it, and she fell over it to the floor.

Kansas gave no thought to Pecos or the gun in his hand. He sprang after her and kicked her in the stomach. She managed to wrap her arms around his knees. He booted her away while Pecos tried to get past the table and the overturned chairs.

He'd have killed her under the hard heels of his boots, but Pecos grabbed him and flung him against the wall. Kansas started back with his left hand outstretched, his right on the butt of his .45. But the gun in Pecos's hand stopped him.

Kansas got his breath. Exertion had burned out some of his rage. He forked a lock of curly hair away from his forehead, jerked out a laugh, and said: "Maybe you think you're taking her over."

"I might."

"No, I like you too well. I even like the Spaniard too well."

Honeyjo was on her knees. She panted and caught her breath, but she wasn't crying. Only cat-like fury showed on her face. She hissed: "I'll kill you! And I'll kill that other woman!"

He bent over, grabbed her by the bodice of her dress, struck her with the heel of his palm, knocking her halfway through the door.

Hernandez was there. He tried to catch her. The force of her knocked him backward. He started for his gun, but Pecos cried: "No!"

Hernandez checked himself. He looked both ways, saw Hoss McFadden with a gun drawn, and Legless Joe Hames leaning against the wall, his Sharps rifle up and ready.

"Eh? You need all these guns to beat one poor woman?"

McFadden said: "All right, greaser. You may be considerable of a lead merchant in your parts, but these ain't your parts. They're ourn. So keep your hands clear of that gun or I'll hit you with this Forty-Five and turn you so's the hair side's in."

The Pecos Kid said—"Let's get out of here."—and led Hernandez across the street.

VI

"Rendezvous at Trapper Springs"

Pecos slept in a room above the Red Flag. Next day he heard
that Honeyjo had been put aboard a river steamer bound for
Benton, but that night, on entering his room, he knew she was
there, close, in the darkness, waiting for him.

He closed the door and stood with his back against it. The
odor of French perfume was heavy on the air. He took a step,
reaching out, expecting to find her.

Then her husky voice came, unexpectedly, behind him.
"Yo' alone?"

"Yes."

"Light a match. I got the window shaded."

He struck the match, lighted a stub of candle. She stood
beside the door, the little dagger still in her hand. She wore a
black dress, drenched and clinging. It had been torn by
brush; its seams had collected cockleburrs and little, sticky
seed balls of sage.

He said: "I thought you'd be twenty miles toward Benton."

She laughed and said: "Lot o' people think they know all
about Honeyjo. They wrong. Nobody know what Honeyjo
will do. Honeyjo had to come back and see you."

"Thanks. But what's the *real* reason?"

"Maybe I'd like to see yo' kill Jack Kansas."

"You do your own killing. I got nothing against Kansas."

"No-o?" She kept smiling. She got his tobacco and papers,
rolled a cigarette, and leaned with the candlelight strong

against her face to light it. "Maybe yo' better kill Kansas befo' he kill you."

"What do you mean?"

"Nothin'. I just tell yo' that little bit."

He grabbed her by the arm and spun her around. *"What do you mean?"*

"Yo' leave me alone. I'll let out a yell, and you'll wish you left me alone. They come up here and fin' me here . . . what they goin' to think? They'll think you got me back after Kansas sent me away."

"What have you got against him?"

"Why yo' think?" She tossed her head back, a vindictive movement. "Yo' think any woman likes to be second best? Well, some women, maybe, not Honeyjo! Honeyjo never be second best!"

"Who was it? That girl of Robin's?"

"Her? No. I'll tell yo' who! That   girl. That girl from yonder." She jerked her head toward the west.

"What's her name?"

"I don't know. I never found out her name. I knew he was seein' somebody. I could smell her perfume every time he got back. He'd take a long ride, to meet some o' them Dakota rustlers . . . he said . . . but when he came back, he smelled, and it wasn't no rustler smell. Laws, I been around heah long enough to know rustler smell."

"That's what you came back to tell me?"

"Yeah."

"Didn't you follow him?"

"I followed him. Found out where he went. Yonder, over west, to that little cabin at Trapper Spring. It was after night, and I didn't git close enough to see who she was, only she left ridin' side-saddle, like a lady. Like a lady from one o' the big ranches."

"You know who she is!"

"No!" She backed off from him, her hand under her dress, once again on the dagger. "Don't get rough with Honeyjo! Honeyjo will . . . !"

"Why'd you think gave a damn whether he had a woman from one of the big ranches?"

She laughed with a toss of her dark ringlets. "Yo' be interested, all right. Yo' interested in everything that Kansas does. I reckon yo'd like to know how he's always ready and mo' than ready when them cattlemen yonder decide they'll clean out Bull Sink. Honeyjo's mighty smart gal. Honeyjo finds out things. You tread easy here, boy, or one o' your steps will land yo' in a hole six feet deep, and they'll be throwin' dirt in your face. Now I've said all I'm going to. I'm leaving. Horseback. And yo' gettin' the horse fo' me."

He grabbed her wrist: "How much does Kansas know?"

"He don' know as much as Honeyjo, or you wouldn't even be alive."

With a downward twist she got away. He made another grab for her and missed. She blew out the candle. She wasn't where he expected. He heard her laugh; the drape was torn off the window; he saw her silhouetted against the moonlight from outside.

She said: "Use yo' head, boy, somebody'll hear us."

She slid outside, hung for a second with her legs dangling, her hands on the sill. Then, wrapping her dress to keep it from catching, she dropped, and he could hear the soft thud of her feet striking the ground.

A second later he dropped from the window after her. It was unfamiliar ground. His high-heeled boots made him fall.

She got hold of him and said: "Where's yo' horse?"

He took her around to the stable. The hostler, a big, half-witted boy, was asleep in the oat bin. No one else around.

Working quietly, he saddled a chestnut horse and led him out.

"Yo' crazy? That's Kansas's favorite bronc'."

"Nothing's too good for you, Honeyjo. Now tell me just how much Kansas knows."

She got one foot in the stirrup, smiled with a flash of her teeth, and whispered: "One thing . . . he don' know as much as Honeyjo. No damn' man know as much as Honeyjo. Got to say good bye now. Yo' look me up sometime in Fo't Benton, boy. Yo' do that if yo' still alive."

The horse was willing to run, and she let him, hitting the rough, winding alley at a gallop.

The hostler still snored. Someone had opened the rear door of the Red Flag, and he could hear Wattles singing "The Night Fair Charlotte Froze to Death by the Dreary Mountainside."

The door closed again, and he knew it was Hernandez.

"Butch!"

"Eh, you, Keed. It was a very peculiar theeng. I was upstairs, to your room, where there is nothing but the smell of French perfume. I would almost think that girl did not leave on the steamboat, after all."

"Butch, a man needs something besides a guitar and a stick of mustache wax to attract women. Me, now . . . I just kick 'em and leave 'em, and they still swim rivers to get to me."

There was commotion in the morning over the theft of the horse, but no one thought of questioning Pecos. Later, visiting the barn to feed his own horse, he found the hostler cowering in the oat bin, his face, neck, and shoulders bloody from a whip-lashing.

Pecos's face looked lean, and he fought down an angry

169

tremble when he asked: "Who quirted you?"

"I ain't telling anything. They'd only whip me some more."

Later he learned that the quirting had been administered by Hoss McFadden. It made him a little sick. He felt to blame because of the hostler, but there was nothing he could do.

He was seated before the Chicago Bar, hat over his eyes, apparently asleep when Jim hunted him out.

"See what they did to that poor, feeble-minded kid?"

He opened his eyes and barked: "Well, why come to me? There's nothing I can do about it."

"Say, you're ringy this morning."

Pecos said—"Sorry."—and, after looking around to make sure no one was in earshot, he told about Honeyjo's visit of the night before.

With alarm in his eyes, Jim said: "She must have an idea we're working for Jawn Ridley. We better get out o' here."

"It'd be sensible."

"I'll find Butch right now."

"I just said it'd be sensible. You go and take Butch if you like, but I'll stay for a while. Thought I might sort of trail over to Trapper Springs." He laughed at Big Jim who was trying to watch both ways down the street at once. "Hell, Jim, if Kansas had an idea we were working for Ridley, we'd have no more to worry about . . . we'd be dead."

He sat through the heat of afternoon, rousing only to roll a cigarette, or brush away the bulldog flies that had become numerous and sticky with the advent of hot weather. The town remained quiet. He ate supper at Big Jim's grub pile, and returned after sunset. A two-bit monte game had finally broken up, and one of the participants, a filthy, lousy old wolfer, bummed him for tobacco and papers. He stopped scratching long enough to roll one and said: "They'll be hell amongst the squaws tonight. Clode Hattersly just came in from Trapper Springs."

Pecos thought little about it until he noticed three riders heading down one of the back trails from town. Twilight prevented him being sure, but he had a strong hunch that one of the three of them was Jack Kansas.

Pecos saddled his horse and set out at an easy amble, apparently headed toward the steamboat landing, but when the town was out of sight, he spurred at an alternate trot and gallop up the big cottonwood-filled coulée that would lead him to Trapper Springs.

He saw nothing of Kansas or the other two. The moon came up. He hunted a way along the cutbank sides, through buckbrush and rose thorns. He traveled steadily for better than an hour. Ahead of him the coulée narrowed with walls of sheer sandrock, forcing him back to the main trail.

He'd never been to Trapper Springs, but it had been described to him, and he knew it was just ahead. On the night breeze he could smell the damp clay and swamp odors of a spring hole. He moved slowly, through huge boulders, hunting their shadows.

Pecos dismounted, removed his spurs, led his horse across treacherous footing, among angular boulders big as cabins. He tied the reins to a juniper trunk, and climbed on. He was careful to keep his heels from scraping the rock. He hunted shadows where there were shadows, ran in swift silence where there wasn't.

Thickets of bullberries choked the narrows giving concealment. He had to crawl on hands and knees. Then there was yielding clay underfoot, and he had his first look at the springs.

The coulée bottom was quite flat, an eighth of a mile in width, and about a mile in length. There was a cabin and some corrals below and to his right. He got down, concealed by some sage clumps, and watched the cabin.

Someone was moving. It was Jack Kansas, on foot, walking up from the spongy bottoms of a little creek, approaching the cabin.

Pecos followed, staying with the creekbank. He lost sight of him beyond the corrals. He watched, but Kansas didn't reappear.

The uphill corner of a corral checked him. Below, among box elder trees, he could see part of the cabin roof. He sat down, slid beneath the fence, kept sliding, digging in the heels of his boots, and stopped against the inner wall of the corral.

He remained on one knee, and listened. After what seemed to be a long wait, he heard the jingle of spurs, and someone approached the house. A door creaked on wooden hinges, and a second later a girl spoke.

"Hello, Kansas."

He had expected it, and yet it was a shock that hit him hard—the voice belonged to Letty Stinchfield.

Pecos cursed through his teeth. He stood up, looking for them through the corral poles. Brush and trees were in the way. He moved along until there was an opening, and he had a view of one side of the cabin and of the path leading up from the creek.

They were there, two shadows, the girl close to the cabin, standing still, Kansas climbing the path. She had on a riding skirt, perhaps the same one she'd worn that night at The Citadel. She was taller and slimmer than he remembered. She waited for Kansas, standing straight, her head up, her shoulders back, her hands braced on her hips.

"So you send for me!" Kansas said with a laugh, and Pecos knew by the tone that she must have sworn *never* to send for him.

She jerked her head and said: "I came to find out about that bay horse of mine. I never sent for you."

Kansas laughed. "Now, darling, that's a pretty poor story."

He took another stride, covering the distance between them, caught her with his left arm around the small of her back, and drew her to him.

She bent back. Their faces were close together for a few seconds. He tried to kiss her, but she turned her head sharply. Moonlight revealed her expression. She was smiling, defiant, and contemptuous. She tried to get out of his grasp, but he'd expected that, and had drawn her arm in a hammerlock.

"You rode a long way, darling. You rode too far to fight very hard. You been dreaming about this every night for a month, why don't you admit it?"

He kept laughing, backing with her as she struggled to get away, putting enough pressure on the hammerlock to *keep* her from getting away.

They were out of Pecos's sight, but he could still hear them, the scrape of their feet, their quick breathing. It was quiet for a second, and he heard the creak and drag of the door. He thought they were inside, but soon he heard them talking. Kansas was still teasing her, the girl panting from effort, speaking through her teeth.

They were quiet then. He listened for what seemed to be a long time. He climbed the fence, dropped to the other side, found a crooked little path down the slope through dwarfed, wide-branching box elder trees.

Now he could hear the girl again. He thought for a second she was crying. She wasn't. She was laughing. They were barely visible against the log wall of the cabin. Jack Kansas had backed her there. He'd dropped the hammerlock. He had one hand braced on each side of her, and, when she tried to

173

move one way or the other, he lowered that arm to stop her. He kept talking in her ear, and she kept laughing.

He forced himself to stand still and listen. He had a job to do for Jawn Ridley. He was doing his job now. He had little doubt that she was the one who kept Kansas informed of everything at The Citadel.

She was doing the talking, and Kansas, with his ear bent close to her lips, was listening. Her voice was something less than a whisper. Pecos picked up a word or two at random, but they told him nothing.

Kansas had hold of her again, and she was fighting him off. Before, her struggle had been half-hearted. But not now. This was the real thing. She fought with teeth and claw, with the savage fury of a lynx cat.

Kansas held her as she twisted halfway around. She fell, and he was on one knee, bent over her. He made a grab as she got away. She turned over. She was in a half-sitting position, one leg stretched out, the other bent beneath her. Her riding skirt was made with wings like a pair of chaps, and these, twisting around her legs, tangled her movements, momentarily tied her down. He bent to grab her, and stopped. Moonlight made a little, steely gleam on the object in her hand. It was the double Derringer.

Kansas managed to laugh. "You wouldn't shoot me."

She hissed: "Get back!"

"Here, girl. Give it to me. Come on, give it to me. Little girls shouldn't play with weapons." As he talked, he edged closer. He raised his voice: "I said . . . give it to me!"

"Get away!"

"No, darlin'. . . ."

He started to grab, and the little gun roared, throwing flame and lead from close range. The slug hit him. It knocked him a quarter way around. He grabbed some projecting logs by the door and saved himself from falling. By his posture Pecos knew he'd been hit in the left arm.

"You hellcat! I should kill you. Woman or not. . . ."

"Keep away from your gun."

She meant it. He didn't follow her farther. Her horse was among the box elder trees. He cursed her as she galloped off. He kept cursing as Hoss McFadden and the other man came up from the creek. "I can catch her, Jack," Hoss said.

"Let her go. Catching her is a job I'll keep for myself."

"Tonight?"

"Tonight? Hell, no. I took a slug in the arm. Here . . . scratch a match and let's have a look at it."

VII

"Unmasked"

Pecos, after hard riding, entered Bull Sink by one of the side trails. He pulled the saddle off his tired mount, and put it on a fresh one from Kansas's string. Then he walked around to the main street looking for Hernandez and Big Jim.

Big Jim saw him and came clumping with long strides from the Chicago Bar. "Kid! I'm glad to see you. We got to hammer some brains into that Mexican's head. You know what he's up to now?"

"I'd lay gold against Jeff Davis dollars he's chasing women."

"He's after that gal o' Robin's and so's that Dakota rustler, Celden Frye."

"You better worry about Frye. Maybe you haven't noticed, but Butch is what I'd call nifty with a gun."

"Frye's got men backing him. Sometimes I almost wish Butch would get a bullet through him, not serious, o' course, but enough to teach him a lesson. I seen men foolish about women, but Butch. . . ."

Big Jim had been steering across to the Red Flag.

"Is he in here?"

"I suppose."

Legless Joe Hames, propped on his Sharps rifle, was near the door, chewing tobacco, watching them. They asked about Hernandez, and he spat on the floor and answered: "Ain't seen him."

Jim said: "He's in this place!"

Hames shifted his weight off the Sharps and raised his voice. "Well, find him yourself."

Pecos pulled Big Jim along, saying: "Don't argue. We'll look upstairs."

Climbing, Jim said: "So you *are* worried about Butch!"

They walked from one door to another, beating on the panels, opening them when no one answered. No sign of him.

They went back to the street, and from place to place, still without finding any trail of him.

Pecos said: "You don't suppose he's at one of those Gros Ventre teepees?"

"Not Butch. He wouldn't. . . ."

"He'd do anything."

A half-breed boy came across the street on silent moccasins and stood looking at them with his dark eyes. "For four bits I will show you where the Spaniard is."

Pecos flipped him the coin. "See? What'd I tell you? He's over with the Gros Ventres, and, if he ends up lousy, he'll be looking for a new partner."

The half-breed, however, took them in the opposite direction from the Indian camp, around shacks and sheds, across bottle heaps to the rear door of the Red Flag.

"We came out o' there not fifteen minutes ago."

The half-breed, without seeming to hear him, led him up the stairs to the one door they had not tried—the one leading to Jack Kansas's room.

He rapped and said: "Me . . . Joe."

The door opened instantly. It was Jack Kansas. The kid jumped out of the way, and they could see that Kansas had a sawed-off shotgun hooked under his arm, aimed, the hammers back.

"Don't try it, boys," he said. "There's a man behind you."

"Yeah, you're damned right there is." Hoss McFadden had been standing in the dim end of the hall. Now he plodded up with a .45 in each hand. "Just keep walkin'. Go inside. The Mex is waitin' for you."

Kansas moved to let them through the doorway. His left shirt sleeve was stained with blood. He still had his spurs on; the saddle wrinkles hadn't yet shaken from his wool pants. Apparently he'd dismounted only minutes before.

Pecos walked so close the muzzle of the shotgun brushed his arm, and he saw Hernandez seated with his boots on the edge of the table, grinning at them.

"So, *señores*, you are out trying to break up the love affairs of your Hernandez one time too many! Behold the buxom beauty I make love to thees night!"

He gestured at a chinless little man with a pimply face and a nose like a tomahawk who sat against the wall covering him with a Colt revolver.

Pecos laughed, sounding easy about it, and drawled: "Why, you're in an even worse fix than usual."

"*Sí,* and thees time it is not of my doing. Not *my* woman. It was *your* woman, that Honeyjo weeth her steenking French perfume. Now pay the man for his horse you stole for her so he will free us of our imprisonment."

Kansas had followed them in. He said: "I'm glad to know where the horse went to, but I'm afraid there's still a couple things that have to be cleared up." Reaching around from behind, he took Pecos's gun, and then Big Jim's, and tossed them on the couch. He was smiling in a knowing, unpleasant way. "Thing I'd like to know is this . . . what's the *real* reason you came down here to the sink?"

"Why, you remember. We were broke. We had a few head of cows. After selling 'em to you, we were still broke."

"Nobody sent you down here? Jawn Ridley, for instance?"

"Now what gave you an idea like that?"

Kansas wasn't in a good mood. Each time he moved his wounded left arm, he winced. "Don't get too smart. I knew somebody'd been staked out here, spying on us. And now I know who it is. It's you."

"I don't reckon you do. If you did, you wouldn't give us a chance to plead innocent. You'd just have shot us when we came up the stairs."

"You were all the way north to Milk River. Then you turned around and came back. You rode straight to The Citadel. No use of denying it. I know you did."

"Of course we did. That was the only ferry that wasn't washed out. And they always feed a drifter at Ridley's. Don't you reckon that's reason enough?"

Hoss shouted: "It's reason enough for us!"

A long stride had brought Hoss up behind him. He knew the blow was coming and tried to turn. The barrel of a gun clipped him on the skull. It was like an explosion inside his brain. He was down, the slivery floor under his hands. He reached, got hold of the table, pulled himself to his knees.

Hoss was still behind him. "Should I let him have another?"

Kansas said: "Wait. Maybe he's ready to talk. How about it, Pecos? Would you rather tell your story or have your skull caved in?"

Pecos said: "I need a drink."

Hoss walked around him, put one of his guns away, poured whisky in a tincup, and threw it in his face.

It blinded him. He wiped it away with his shirt sleeve. He kept wiping it away, pretending to be blinded after things became visible.

Hernandez was still at the edge of his chair, the pimply-faced man's gun in his back. Kansas had turned his shotgun on Big Jim who'd retreated a couple of steps toward the wall.

Their six-guns lay on the couch where Kansas had put them. They were only a long dive and grab away, but he'd be a dead man if he tried to make a play for them.

Kansas was saying: "Live or die, Kid. Up to you."

"What?"

"Pour him a drink, Hoss. And this time let him drink it."

Pecos said: "I need a smoke."

"All right, have a smoke."

They watched Pecos get tobacco and papers out of his pocket. He rolled one, licked it into shape. He had his mind on reaching for the lamp, but Kansas was wary for tricks.

"None o' that, Kid. You might get foolish. The second you tried to dump that lamp I'd kill you. Then you'd never get your story told, and I'd never hear it."

Hoss said: "Just stay put. I'll light it for you." He lifted the lamp, held it by its bowl, tilted it so the chimney was beneath the tip of the cigarette.

Pecos only had to drag to get it lighted. He still seemed to be groggy. He kept shaking his head. He took the cigarette from his lips. "You knocked one of my teeth loose."

"From behind? How in hell could I 'a' done that?"

Pecos bared his teeth, and, as Hoss looked, he laid the coal of his cigarette on the back of his hand. It took a half second for pain to hit him. The big man yelled and started back, still holding the lamp. Pecos's toe was behind his boot heel, and he fell. The lamp struck the floor. The chimney broke, but not the bowl.

Pecos dived forward. The air was ripped by flame and explosion. Both barrels of the sawed-off. He could feel the wind whip of flying buckshot, the splinter and thud as it tore into the wall. He reached the couch. The guns were there. His hands found them, and he rolled over with a gun in each hand. He fired. The buck and roar felt good to him. The

180

room rocked with a blazing crossfire. Then it stopped.

Flame still clung to the wick of the upset lamp. It looked brownish through the powder smoke. He'd had an impression of men charging for cover, of a man falling, of someone diving through the open window. He got to his feet. He moved along with the wall at his back. The side of one foot touched something yielding and heavy. A man's body.

Suddenly, sick-frightened, he said: "Butch!"

Men were struggling. He could feel the heavy shifting of weight, labored grunting. They fell with a crash over chairs.

Hoss's voice: "Damn it, you're breakin' my arm."

Big Jim: "Stand up!"

"Yeah."

"Open the door."

The lamp flame was now racing along cracks in the floor where the kerosene had flowed.

Pecos whispered louder: "Butch!"

An answering came from an unexpected direction. "Here, *señor!*"

Relief at finding him alive made Pecos want to laugh and cry at the same time. "We got to get the hell out of here."

"*Sí,* and queeck."

Firelight revealed the body of the skinny, pimply man, face down, his arms spread-eagled, a dark smear of blood under his left side. No sign of Kansas. It had been Kansas who'd gone through the window.

Men had been shouting in the saloon below. Now they were pouring up the stairs. They were in the hall like a cattle stampede.

Big Jim, with McFadden's two arms in a double hammer-lock, had forced him to the door.

Pecos cried: "No, Jim. It's no use. It'll have to be the window."

Hernandez said: "Where is that peeg, Kansas? Did we not kill him?"

Pecos was at the window. The flames silhouetted him. From below came twin flashes of explosion. A bullet carved the window casing by his waist; another shattered the glass over his head and stung him with flying fragments.

He fired back, and went for cover. The room was suffocating with heat and the raw stench of burning oil.

Hernandez, choking, gasped: "Thees is one hell of a place you got us into, Keed."

"I got you into? If you hadn't been chasing that woman of Robin's. . . ." He didn't have the breath left to finish it. He started to cough and couldn't stop. It made his lungs raw. "Get out!" he gasped. "Jim, get out. The window. I'll cover you!"

Jim let go his hammerlock and came across the room. A gargantuan figure, he stumbled over a chair. He grabbed the windowsill and took a massive breath.

"Get out!" Pecos shouted.

Big Jim started head foremost through the opening. Balanced with head and shoulders down, he clawed for handholds without finding them. Pecos grabbed him by his thighs and dumped him overboard.

They were shooting from below, and he fired back. His guns were empty. "Butch! Where are you? Get out o' here."

"The hell weeth you, *senor*. It is your turn."

"*I* ain't arguing!" Hoss McFadden bellowed and charged past. A bullet hit him. He grunted as though he'd been struck by a sledge. He held for a second to the window casing, then his fingers gave way, and he fell headfirst toward the ground. Pecos went through after Hoss, with Hernandez close behind.

Pecos picked himself up from the ground. Pain knifed

through his foot and up his leg.

"Where's Jeem?" Hernandez whispered.

Jim was only a couple of steps away. "Here I am. I feel like my neck was broke."

Pecos got himself balanced against the wall. He'd turned his ankle. He was trying his weight on it. "We got to get to the corral."

Light from the flaming window suddenly struck them. They crawled to the concealment of a rubbish heap, on to some sheds, and to the corral.

The half-witted boy was cowering in the oat bin. Pecos stuck an empty gun in his face and shouted the single word: "Horses!"

Pecos followed him outside, fingering cartridges from his belt, feeding them into the cylinder of a .45.

Jim grabbed him: "Give me my gun."

"Help the kid. I'll do the shooting."

Flames now poured from the upper window of the Red Flag. They burst through the roof. They raced through the flimsy, dried-out building. It created a roaring draft. The building was a torch, lighting the ground for a hundred yards around with the brightness of sunrise.

"Horses!" Big Jim was bellowing. "Damn it, didn't you want horses?"

They ran across the corral where wild bullets cut furrows through dusty hoof-trodden manure. Jim and the hostler were holding three horses.

"Mine's saddled, back of that shed," Pecos said.

"Hell of a time to tell us."

"Maybe we'll need an extra one the way the lead's flying."

They rode out at a gallop, hunting the long shadows of buildings. There was no sound of pursuit. After a mile Hernandez drew to a sliding halt and cried: "My guitar! Oh, my sweetheart, how could I leave you behind in that dive, Dinny's Chicago Bar? *Señores,* do not try to stop me. I must return for my guitar."

"Let him go," Pecos said, getting hold of Big Jim's bridle. "He'll come back all right. You know what the Blackfeet say about crazy men . . . the Lord watches over them."

"They'll kill him!"

"No, he's got the word of a Gypsy they won't. Don't you remember? Butch is going to die of rheumatics at the age of eighty-five."

They rode slowly to the springs where they'd camped that first night. The air was cool, and very clear. Across the miles separating them from Bull Sink came the occasional high-pitched sounds of men's voices. A glow of fire was still in the sky. It slowly died. Then, after long waiting, there was an-other sound—a voice backed by the soft rhythm of a guitar. It was Hernandez, singing.

> **¡Ay, ay, ay, ay!**
> **Canta y no llores. . . .**

"You see?" Pecos said. "The Blackfeet are right."

They rode through night and dawn, and morning heat. The homestead shack had an abandoned, dismal look even in the brilliant light of afternoon. They stopped to graze their horses and sleep for a few hours, and awoke with the sun dropping toward the horizon.

Cursing the pack rats that had made off with both bacon and jerky, Big Jim stirred up a mess of plain flour and salt dough-gods.

"We still homesteaders?" Hernandez asked.

Pecos said: "Oh, hell, no. It was a bum idea from the start.

Kansas knows who we're working for. These Union sodbusters will know, too, as soon as one of 'em visits Bull Sink. Best we can do is drift back to The Citadel and break the news to Jawn Ridley."

VIII

"Jawn Ridley's Son"

At The Citadel, Jawn Ridley heard Pecos's story with his heavy jaw set, a steady frown on his face. He lighted a Havana cigar and walked off, leaving its rich fragrance behind. From the bay window he had a view of jackpine hills, of terraces, of limitless prairie benches dropping one after another toward the Big Dry—all part of his domain.

Pecos said: "I was high-carded, but they did it with a marked deck."

"Sure, sure. Not blaming you, Major. In fact, I think you did very well. You're sure it was safe for you to come back here in broad daylight?"

"Thinking of those sodbusters? They'll know we work for you next visit they make to Bull Sink."

"Sure, sure. Still, your mission wasn't exactly fruitless. Glass of something? Sherry? Brandy?"

Ridley's mind was on other things, Pecos could tell that by his eyes. He seemed little interested in things at Bull Sink. Once before Pecos had had the impression that Ridley cared little whether he cleaned out the rustlers or not. After all, they had little to do with cattle, and their horse exchange business hurt Wyoming and Dakota raisers more than they did outfits like Ridley's and Stinchfield's that were close at hand.

"A marked deck," Ridley repeated, talking Havana smoke from his mouth. He stood with his powerful legs wide set, his hands clasped behind him. A finely wrought, ivory-handled gun of some unfamiliar make was strapped high around his waist, carried in a cut-away holster, and Pecos found himself wondering how well Ridley could go for it, and deciding that he could probably go for it well, indeed, like he went for everything else he wanted. "Marked deck. Yes, that's an apt term. Trust a Confederate to find an apt term. These Yankees. . . ." He called them a vile name. "They'll not slice up my range and brand my cattle for the benefit of those brigands at Bull Sink!"

"Seh, according to my observation, they're not."

He whirled, and for the first time fury showed on his face. "Whose side are you on?"

"Why, up till now I reckoned it was your side."

"Up till *now?*"

"I went yonder to find out who was informing against us at Bull Sink, and who was furnishing the cattle that kept those boys in business."

"Oh. Sure, sure. Sorry, Major. Well, who *is* informing against us at Bull Sink?"

"I don't know."

He laughed with a surprised, half-contemptuous jerk of his head. "You still haven't got an idea?"

"I got an almighty good idea, but I'm not saying till I'm sure. That's for your good as well as anyone else's."

"*My* good." He opened his eyes, and there was a hint of a smile on his lips. "For instance, my own son?" Then he shook it off. "No, it wouldn't be Albert." He walked to the massive mahogany table and drove his fist on it so hard the humidor of cigars jumped an inch. "My God, man, how I wish he did have guts enough! I'd rather he'd be a traitor than what he is. At least, a traitor sometimes has the guts of a man."

"Oh come, seh, I'm sure the boy. . . ."

"You don't need to save my feelings. You know what the

187

boy is. You knew from the first night. Piano player, scribbler. And the joke is, I built all this for him."

"He's still a boy."

"At his age I rode in the cavalry with a cutlass in my hand, and so did you. I have 'punchers his age who have ridden the long trail from Texas."

"He'll still be a boy if you never give him a chance to grow up."

"*I have* given him his chance. And I'll give him more chances. He'll not go to Saint Louis. His mother can go to Saint Louis if she wants, but *he'll stay here*. I'll make a man of him yet. I'll make a man of him, or kill him. Does that sound like an unnatural way for a father to talk? I still say it. *I'll make a man of him, or kill him*."

Pecos went outside. A man stood on the porch, one boot propped on the rail, staring off toward the river. He carried a brace of .45s low and tied down to his thighs. The silver conchos on his belt told Pecos that this was the same tall gunman who'd been in that exact spot when he emerged from Ridley's office the first night.

"You always stand there, seh?" he said in his easy drawl.

The man turned abruptly. He looked at Pecos with narrowed eyes. He had buck teeth and a loose underjaw. There was something subnormal about his expression, yet his eyes had an animal intelligence, like a weasel's. "If I want to stand here, I guess that's my business."

"Yours and Ridley's. No offense. I just like to pass the time of day. I'm called the Pecos Kid." His eyes traveled to the open window just behind them. He had a hunch the man had been listening, and that he'd been listening the other night. "But I'd wager you knew already."

The man didn't catch the significance of the remark. He said: "Yeah, I knew already." He got the band of his pants and his two gun belts in one movement, hitching up all of them. "My name's Garde. Carris Garde." He twisted his loose jaw in a smile. "Maybe you heard o' *me*, too."

"Should I have?"

Pecos walked on. He didn't like him, and he didn't pretend to like him. Carris Garde. He kept repeating the name as he walked down, past the bunkhouses. He couldn't remember where he'd heard it before.

A young wrangler was inside one of the corrals, preparing to take the rough spots off a sorrel broncho. Pecos saw Hernandez, climbed to the corral beside him, and asked: "You ever heard of a gunman named Carris Garde?"

"The two-gun man of the beeg house? *Si*. From Utah. I have heard he killed five men. He was a deputy under Sampson at Silver City. But Sampson had to get rid of him. Sometimes Sampson wished to arrest a man *alive*, while Carris would always bring them in dead."

"I suppose he just walked up and said . . . *Go for your guns*. And then, *wham!*"

Hernandez laughed with a flash of his white teeth. "Or else, because of his great kindness, he just shot them in the back. *¿Quién sabe?*" He pointed his cigarette at the broncho that had just tossed his rider and was sunfishing around, kicking dirt in his face. "If *Señor* Ridley would let me add thees fine sorrel to my string, perhaps I would go in there and show that boy how a rough horse should be smoothed off. What you theenk?"

"You stay where y'are. You'll break your greaser neck."

"*Si*. You talked me out of it." He pointed with his cigarette and said: "There's the poet."

Albert Ridley had climbed the corral across from them. He looked more boyish than that first night. He'd be a big man someday, but he was developing late and still lacked coordination. He seemed ill at ease and apologetic. The boys had been shouting and laughing as the sorrel bucked around the corral, but now they fell silent.

"I feel sorry for the kid," Pecos said.

"Sorry? Ha! What fool talk is thees? Why would you feel sorry for a man who is due to inherit a cattle empire and perhaps marry the most beautiful girl in all the land? If you have sorrow, give some of eet to me, your friend who love you. Your Hernandez who is tail over teakettle in debt, a strange man in a strange land, without a pot to make coffee in or a window to throw it out of."

The sorrel had come to a stop with flanks quivering, eyes wild, nostrils out. One of the cowboys, with a grin and a wink to his companion, said: "How about it, Al? You like to rub a couple of spots off this sorrel?"

Everybody was watching Al Ridley then. He knew it. He seemed very lonely, there on the top rail.

Pecos said: "They'd like to get him killed."

"Eh? No chance. He'll not get on the horse."

"Want to bet?"

"¡Si! Here is where I reduce my debts to the tune of five thousand dollars. Five thousand he will never touch the hair of that horse."

Albert must have heard him. He moved suddenly, sliding down inside the corral. Anger clearly showed in the twitch of his lips. "Yes, I'll try."

Nobody made a move. Now that he'd accepted, they were afraid of the consequences. They had contempt for the boy, but they were also fearful of his father.

Pecos swung over and jumped to the ground. "It's all right, boys," he said, ambling across. "Al, here, says he'll fork that broncho, and he'll do it."

The horse wrangler, a tall, tow-headed fellow about Al

Ridley's age, had the sorrel by the hackamore and led him over to the fence. There the sorrel fought him, reared, tried to tramp him under his front hoofs. Finally, with the help of two other cowboys, he got the animal snubbed close to the fence with a big, cotton kerchief over his eyes for a blindfold.

Al Ridley hadn't said a word. Pecos, beside him, could see the tremble of the tense muscles around his lips.

"Scared?" Pecos asked.

"I'll get thrown. I'm no rider."

"Wrangler got thrown, too. So what the hell?"

"You'll lose your five thousand," Ridley said.

"I ain't got five thousand. Me or that Spik-Mick, neither one. What's more, we never will have as long as there's poker, whisky, and women in the territory. It's all I.O.U. Now you go ahead and fork that broncho."

The broncho, blindfolded, didn't realize the rider was there until he felt pressure in the stirrup. He ripped back and hammered his front hoofs against the corral poles. That gave him the purchase he needed, and he pulled away. The hackamore rope was dragging. Young Ridley was in the saddle, leaning forward, trying to get it.

"Whitey, hand him the rope!" somebody shouted, but Whitey, the wrangler, was on the run. Ridley got hold of it as the broncho shook off the blindfold, pivoted, and went squealing and sunfishing into the air. He lasted that jump and the next. A change in the animal's bucking tempo loosened him in the saddle. He was bucked over the horn. He had a handful of mane. One boot was out of the stirrup, one leg lower than the other. Next jump he was on the ground with the horse bucking over him.

The sorrel didn't step on him. He was a wild horse but not an outlaw. He bucked twice around the enclosure with his head down and stirrups a-whopping. Al was up, trying to wipe manure dust out of his eyes.

"You got sacked, Ridley," the horse wrangler said.

One of the 'punchers said: "What in hell you crowin' about? You got your nose dug in the dirt, too."

Albert discovered he couldn't use his left arm. It was twisted, but not broken. Big Mike Coffey had just ridden in from Benton and was watching from his foreman's house. He called: "Better get him down here before his mother sees him."

"Sorry about the five thousand," Al said.

"Why, that still leaves about fifty-two thousand the Mex owes me."

IX

"Seeds of Suspicion"

Pecos was outside, renewing his acquaintance with Mike Coffey, when a Chinaman came and summoned him to the big house. He expected to be met by Jawn Ridley. Instead, the Chinaman took him up some stairs, and inside a small sitting room. The shades were drawn, and he was blind from the sun. The room had a closed-in smell, an incense, sachet, funeral-parlor smell.

He groped, got hold of a chair, and a woman said in a high, querulous voice: "Ho, don't sit down. Don't touch anything. I don't want to have my things soiled."

She seemed to be riding an emotional knife edge, threatening to slip and become hysterical.

The Chinaman left, closing the door. Slowly the sun flicker left Pecos's eyes, and he could see her. She wasn't young. She was thin, gray, and tall. She was very pale, with spots of color in her cheeks. Once, perhaps, she'd been beautiful.

He bowed and said: "Yes, ma'am."

"I'm Missus Ridley."

"Yes, ma'am."

"What do you mean by making a laughingstock of my boy?"

"Did I, ma'am?"

She raised her voice until it was almost a scream. "Yes, you did! You made a fool of him in front of all those common hired men, and. . . ."

"He didn't make a fool of himself, ma'am. He got on a bad horse and was thrown. He. . . ."

"Don't interrupt me!"

Pecos thought for a second her anger would carry her into a convulsion. It frightened him. He was sweating. He wanted to escape. The air in the room seemed unclean, unfit to breathe. He forced himself to stand still and listen to her.

"You might as well admit it! It wasn't your idea to do that. It was *his*. *His!*"

"Whose, ma'am?"

"My husband's! Jawn Ridley. He'd do anything to win him away from me. He'd even kill him. Yes, he would! I've heard him say so!"

"Ma'am."

"My father . . . do you know who my father was? Colonel Marcus Burnside! He was with Jefferson Davis at the Southern White House in Montgomery. He used to be seated for dinner only two chairs from the President himself. Think of it, *the President!* And now look at me. In this awful place . . . hot and dusty and awful. In this wild country, surrounded by savages. Me and my baby!"

Pecos stood and watched as she wept. Her shoulders poked up like spurs inside her ruffled, lacy dress. There was no meat on her frame at all.

"Ma'am," he said, wanting to do something, but there was nothing he could do. He took half a step and drew back.

She detected the sympathy in his tone and lifted her head. "Do you want to help me? *Do* you?"

"Ma'am. . . ." He didn't know what to say.

"You'll have to help me escape. Yes, *escape*. He's keeping me prisoner here. I keep writing my relatives to come for me, but he destroys the letters."

"I'm sure he doesn't, ma'am. I'm sure you must be mistaken."

She screamed: "Yes, he does! Oh, he'd let *me* go. But I won't go without my boy. He wants to keep him here. He wants to make him marry that vile, shameless woman."

"Letty Stinchfield?"

Mrs. Ridley called the girl names. She called her things that should never have come from a woman's lips. Pecos tried to stop her. When he couldn't, he backed to the door. He opened it, stopped in the hall.

"Good bye, ma'am."

Pecos closed the door. Jawn Ridley was at the head of the stairs. His face looked hollow beneath his high cheek bones and the big ridge of bone over his brow.

"What are you doing there?"

Pecos met his gaze and said: "Seh, she sent for me."

Ridley fought back the words he was about to speak. He took a very deep breath. Then he laughed bitterly. "Behold The Citadel! My happy home! My wife, a crazy invalid with a tongue like a drunken bawd. My son a coward."

"No, he's not a coward."

"You think not? You really think not?"

"I think not. There's only one thing wrong with the boy."

"What?"

"You, seh."

Ridley stood, still filling the stairway, looking into Pecos's eyes. He'd had a powerful grip on the balustrade. Now he noticed he'd torn a piece of it loose. He rammed it back into place and said in a husky voice: "I need a drink. Let's talk about this. You'll stay for supper. I tell you, there's no payment I wouldn't make if you made a man of that boy."

Pecos sat at the table being served by a Chinese waiter.

The waiter was swift and deft and silent. The quality of the food reminded him of the days long ago when he'd been on furlough in New Orleans. Overhead was a three-lamp chandelier with a thousand points of cut-glass glitter. It shone at cross-purposes with the sundown, giving the room a peculiar twilight.

Ridley was at the head of the table, eating, watching his son, watching Letty Stinchfield, who'd ridden up during the late afternoon with her uncle, Dennis, a big, florid man in California trousers and a fancy shirt and vest.

It was Dennis who did the talking, expansive and extremely sure of himself after six trips to the brandy bottle. "It's just a question of time before we have to uproot those nesters, Jawn. It's my considered judgment they're too cowardly to make the first move. No matter what you say, that'll be up to us."

Ridley said: "Dinner time, Dennis. Let's not bring up unpleasant subjects at the dinner table."

Pecos kept watching Letty Stinchfield. Her skin seemed unusually dark by the crosslight. His mind kept going over that scene at Trapper Springs. He didn't like to think of her in Jack Kansas's arms. He didn't like to think of her as the informer, either. He wondered if she was the reason Jawn Ridley changed the subject.

"How's your arm?" she asked Albert.

He was staring at his plate. "It's all right."

"I heard you tried to ride the sorrel."

"I got thrown." Albert looked over at Dennis and said: "What right do you have, or does anyone have, to shoot those nesters off the range? They're grabbing it like you did, and we did."

"See?" Jawn Ridley said. "Didn't I tell you we shouldn't talk about it at the dinner table?"

Afterward, Pecos sat over brandy and cigars with Ridley and Dennis Stinchfield.

Ridley, while in thoughtful scrutiny of the clarity of his drink, said: "I've been informed, Dennis, that I shouldn't talk over our plans while anyone is listening, not even my son. Someone has been carrying our plans to the men down in Bull Sink."

Dennis cried: "Not Albert!"

"And not Letty. But it's just as well to be sure. By the way, Carris Garde was in Miles City eight or nine days ago, hiring men. At eighty a month." He said it significantly. Eighty was double a cowboy's wage and meant only one thing—gunmen. "He came back with four, and there'll be a couple more. I don't want too big an army, but I want it to be select. Carris Garde, the Pecos Kid, Hernandez Flanagan, Jim Swing, Curly Wolfe, Snake River Johnny, Tom Pierce . . . we'll handle the jobs that need to be done. I'm counting on you for half a dozen, Dennis."

"You'll get 'em."

Pecos asked softly: "What do you plan? Direct attack on Bull Sink?"

"To hell with Bull Sink! Burn it out, and it would spring up again before the ashes were cold. If you want to kill the tree, the thing to do is cut its roots. In this case, the source of revenue. Bull Sink's source lies up there on Bull Creek, Horn Creek, and the Sage."

"Those sodbusters?" Pecos scoffed "Oh, hell, Ridley. Bull Sink operates on horses. *Long* horses. Best I could get for rustled cows was a straight five dollars a head, and that was. . . ."

"I wonder," Ridley said with a cold selection of words, "how far a Confederate major had to travel to make him love a bunch of damn' Yankees."

"I traveled a few miles, I did for a fact. For a good many of those miles I fought the wah over again. Then one mawnin' I woke up and noticed that the same sun was shining on all of us, Yankee and Reb, and that we all wanted the same things, good and bad. No, seh, you made a mistake if you brought me down here to fight the Wah for the Southern Confed'racy all over again."

"That mean you wouldn't kick a pack of lousy, range-chopping nesters off my grass?"

"I don't reckon, seh, I'd have much part in it." He stood up. "Sorry, Jawn. I guess it's all been a mistake. You should o' let us just ride on from Milk River to the Sweetgrass."

"Wait. You realize if you quit me now what kind of a light it would place me in? Back at the territorial capital they'd be saying . . . of course, Ridley's in the wrong. The Pecos Kid wouldn't fight for him."

"Sorry, seh."

"What if I proved to you that *you* were wrong? . . . that those nesters under the Rutledge boys and old Gus Hyslop were in business branding my stock?"

"Why, that'd be another matter. I sure as hell would lump 'em with Kansas and the boys at the Sink."

"All right, then, stay for a while. And sit down. Where do you get that vinegar temper? From Tully, your old brigade commander? There was a cavalryman . . . Tully! Let's have a drink to Tully."

X

"The Wheels Start to Turn"

During the late days of June half a dozen eighty-a-month 'punchers arrived from Miles City led by careless, hard-eyed Curly Wolfe. None of them worked. They lay all day in the shade of the bunkhouses, lighting cigarettes that always went out, and had to be lighted again, talking about women and horses, telling interminable lies about their adventures along their back trails.

One of them, a heavy, dirty, whiskered man named Tom Pierce came home from the saloons at Ridley Landing in a bellicose mood one day and, after announcing that he was on the prod hankering to kill a Mex or an Indian, found himself in trouble with Hernandez who shattered first one of his arms, and then the other, as he went for his guns. Pecos heard the shooting and came running in time to apply a tourniquet to Pierce's left arm and save him from bleeding to death.

Pierce kept moaning, cursing, and saying: "I'll kill him, I'll kill him. Git my arms out o' these slings and I'll kill him."

Pecos said dryly: "Looks to me like you got out of it pretty lucky."

"I was drunk. Wait'll I get sober."

"When you're sober, you won't have the guts. Soon as you're on your feet, I'd advise you to head back toward Miles."

Pecos walked from the hot shadow of that bunkhouse and met Carris Garde. Garde had been listening. He smiled with his loose mouth pulled to one side, an unpleasant smile that grated like sand in your food.

Pecos stopped and said: "Bad habit, you got, Carris . . . listening wherever you see an open window."

"Don't tell *me* what to do. I'm telling *you!*"

"Seh?"

"I went all the way to Miles for those men, and I don't want 'em shot up when they get drunk and helpless."

"*You're* not drunk or helpless."

Men along the bunkhouse awning were tense, silent, waiting for his response, expecting a showdown. Carris wanted to save his pride, but he didn't want it to go too far. He swaggered, and made his habitual movement of hitching his trousers and gun belts. "I wouldn't get too ringy, Pecos."

"Why?"

"We both work for the same man."

Pecos laughed and said: "Yeah. You resented me ever since I first rode up here, haven't you?"

"I haven't resented you. You're just another gunman as far as I'm concerned, and so's the Spaniard. But I rode a long way to hire Pierce, in there, and I don't want somebody running him out."

"Then tell him to stay. But I'll wager he won't."

Pecos walked around the corrals to a grove of cottonwoods guided by the soft music of a guitar. Hernandez had his back against a tree, hat over his eyes. He knew who it was without looking and asked: "He will live, Keed?"

"I guess. You better be careful. That's a mean crowd. A back-shootin' crowd."

"Then perhaps more bullets are needed."

"Just stay clear of 'em, that's all."

Hernandez laid the guitar away with a movement of impatience. "For too long we have been in one place. Day after day . . . notheeng. Just sit, sit, sit in the shade, slap at flies, wear the fingers out on a guitar. Talking at the steamboat landing, I heard of a great silver strike in Idaho. A boom town, like Butte, weeth more money, money, money everywhere. In thees boom town, there is a music-house hotel four stories high, a skyscraper, filled to the roof weeth women. It would be much better than thees, no?"

"Sure, but we dealt ourselves a hand. We'll stay put a while."

"Eh, so." Hernandez heaved a deep sigh and laid back again. "What happened at that meeting last night?"

"What meeting?"

One eye appeared from beneath the hat. "Eh? You were not there, at the beeg house, with Jawn Ridley, that fancy Dennis Stinchfield, and Carris Garde? They talked behind your back?"

He thought it over and said: "They might have. I got a good nose, Butch, just like you. I been smelling something lately."

A week passed. Each day the Pecos Kid rode with Albert Ridley, getting the young fellow to talk, to tell about his troubles. He taught him things about riding, tracking, and shooting.

One night he returned and found the shades of Ridley's office drawn, a light shining behind them, and a couple of Stinchfield horses tied in the shed adjoining the carriage house.

He walked around the back way, and stepped quietly to the porch. He stood still, listening. The heavy tone of Ridley's voice reached him, but none of the words was audible. He started to go closer, but there was movement near him in the dark. He turned sharply and stood face to face with

Letty Stinchfield. She'd been standing in the shadow of a porch pillar.

She said: "And *you're* the man who accused Carris Garde of eavesdropping!"

"We all do it."

She came toward him. Her head was tilted slightly to one side. She was trying to read his expression in the dark. "Why have you been avoiding me?"

"You don't know when you're lucky." She'd started to put her hands on his shoulders, and he took hold of her wrists, stopping her. "Al is a nice kid. Why don't you marry him?"

"Maybe he's not my idea of a man."

"Who is your idea?"

She ran a soft hand across his shoulder. "Who do you suppose?"

"Maybe Jack Kansas."

She tensed. She stepped back. Her eyes had a trapped look. "Why'd you say that?"

"I was at Trapper Springs one night. You told him about us, didn't you? Why did you try to get us killed?"

"I didn't tell him about you! I didn't tell him anything."

"Looking for a stray horse?" he said, laughing.

"No. No, I wasn't. I just get sick of things here. My uncle, my grandfather, all of them keeping me staked out for Al Ridley. A girl likes to have a fling of her own choosing. But I'm not a spy!"

"Who *has* been carrying information to them?"

She shrugged. "Carris, maybe. It doesn't make much difference *now*."

"What do you mean . . . *now?*"

"Why don't you sleep in the daytime and stay awake at night? It might surprise you to find out who his visitors are." She backed off, shaking her head, her hand inside the bosom of her blouse. "Don't try to make me say any more. I still carry the Derringer. I'll just add this, Mister Pecos . . . why don't you go? Get out. Go where you came from. You're just window dressing for Ridley. He keeps you because of your reputation for fighting on the right side. But one of these days he won't need you any longer. So get out. Get out while you have the chance."

Pecos ate supper with the Ridleys the next night, and found big Jawn to be jovial. Too jovial. Afterward, Pecos climbed to Albert's room, rapped, and went inside, closing the door after him.

"Your dad's turned up some way of driving those Yankee homesteaders off the range, Al?"

Al suddenly had the shakes. Pecos knew how it was—he was scared of his father, yet he considered Pecos his only real friend and wanted to tell the truth. It was cool, with a breeze blowing up from the river, but perspiration gathered in beads on Al's forehead.

Pecos said: "Don't tell me if you don't want to."

"Yes, I'll tell you. Notice you haven't seen Mike Coffey around here lately? Dad's got him reopening the King Midas Mine."

Pecos thought about it and shook his head. "I don't understand."

"He's freighted in a ten-stamp mill and steam engine. Do you know what he's going to grind and dump into the Big Sage? That King Midas vein. Only it's not really a vein, but a fumarole deposit . . . lime, and sulphur and lemon arsenic."

"Why, that'll be slow death to anything drinkin' the water. He'll run his head into territorial law."

Al laughed bitterly and said: "What'll those homesteaders do about it? Complain to Helena where the mining interests have all the power? They might as well complain to the King of England."

Pecos knew it was true. It would do them no more good than it did those ranchers on the Blackfoot who tried legally to prevent the big hydraulic outfits from covering their fields with placer tailings. He said: "No more'n a third of 'em are settled along the Sage."

"Those fumarole deposits crop out for fifteen or eighteen miles. When he's through with the Sage, he can move over the divide and dump them into the tributaries of the Horn."

"And he'll end up by killing his own cattle."

"Dad's sworn to run those Yankee homesteaders off the range, and he'll do it. He'll do it if it costs him every hoof he owns. You don't know my dad like. . . ."

"Yeah, I reckon I do know what he's like. He'll win in spite of hell."

Al saw Pecos was getting ready to leave and looked scared. "Say, you won't tell . . . ?"

"Don't worry about me, Al. You did me a favor in telling me. I'll say nothing about how I found out."

"What are you going to do?"

"Only one thing I can do. I got to ride over to the Sage and talk compromise. You know what'll happen otherwise. They'll go to law about the tailings, and, when that does no good, they'll go for their guns. That'd mean range war. I been in on a couple o' those, and I never saw anybody win, the ones that started 'em, or the ones that finished 'em."

XI

"Compromise or Else"

Starting at dawn, the Pecos Kid followed the southward-trending valley of Ridley Creek until he sighted the yellowish scars of some prospecting dumps high along the ridge. It was a difficult climb through rock and timber, taking until noon. He found that the prospects were shallow and for some years abandoned, but the wind carried an odor of woodsmoke, and, continuing to the crest of the ridge, he got a view of more impressive diggings, of tunnel entrances fronted by big cones of dump rock, of cabins and ore bins, of a shaft with an old horse winch. The woodsmoke came from the chimney of a house a mile farther on where a fresh, pinkish scar ran horizontally along the hill. A large log mill building was about half completed. A trestle and chute ran downhill from the cut, terminating in a bin that from the distance looked like a large, square chimney. Horses and wagons kept creeping up the newly dug road.

Thirst made him look longingly at the tributary of the Big Sage that flowed past the mill, but, instead of riding toward it, he turned at right angles northeastward where, far off, he could see the angular reflections of ranch buildings. If his guess were right, the place belonged to one of the Rutledge boys.

Traveling that way, it was late afternoon before he reached the creek. There it had lost its cold clearness and ran muddy and warm with green scummed banks and the mixed smells of mint and manure. He followed a wagon track past an irrigated field where corn stood high as a man's shoulders. A log house and some sheds came in sight through the box elder trees, and he could see a woman with a forearm shading her eyes watching his approach.

He dismounted to open a gate. A couple of hounds dashed up showing their teeth, but, when he spoke, they lost their ferocity and almost disjointed their rear-ends with wagging. He rode on, up the slight rise, across the hard-beaten dirt of the farmyard. The woman was probably thirty-five, although she looked older. She'd been dried out and beat out by the country. She kept her right arm out of view, inside the door. She had a rifle or a shotgun in there.

"Hello, ma'am," he said, dismounting and taking his hat off. He had a good smile. He limped up on his horse-tired legs, fingering sweaty, brick-colored hair away from his forehead. "I'm mighty thirsty."

"That's a Ridley brand," she said, looking at his horse.

"Yes, ma'am. About me being thirsty. . . ."

"You a Ridley rider?"

"Yes. I work for Ridley. I been yonder." He jerked his head back toward the ridge. "I been riding since mawnin' without water."

He could see movement behind her in the house. A couple of kids were trying to see around her while she pushed them back. Then through the hot air came a burst of galloping hoofs, and she jumped with relief. She came out, dragging with her an old-time percussion shotgun. "Harry!" she shouted to a man just as he came in sight around the sheds.

It was gangling, tall Harry Rutledge mounted bareback on a big-footed work horse. He reined to a jog and came up with his right hand on the butt of the Colt strapped around his waist.

"You!" he said, recognizing Pecos. "What do *you* want?"

"I'm here as a friend, Rutledge."

"Like you was homesteading that Parker place as a friend?"

"I wasn't there to harm you. I was just trying to find out what the deal was in Bull Sink."

Rutledge laughed with a bitter jerk of his head. He didn't dismount. His hands were clenched into fists that looked very large at the ends of his long, skinny arms. He was dressed in a faded patchwork of clothes. His boot heels were run over from following a plow; his sombrero was so old it had lost all semblance of its original shape, but rose to a cone at the crown, and hung in folds so he had to keep his head back in order to see. He kept looking this way and that, along the cutbank rims, and along the creek.

"I'm alone," Pecos said.

"Maybe you are, and maybe you're not. What you here looking for?"

"One thing would be a drink of water."

"Well, you just crossed the crick."

"That's not my idea of drinking water. Seh, in this country you don't even refuse water to your worst enemy."

"I ain't refusin' it. What d'you think *we* drink? Think we got a ice-water spring like up at The Citadel?"

"I'm sorry, seh. I thought. . . ."

"We got some settlings in the barrel," he muttered grudgingly. "Git him a dipperful, Maude."

Maude brought it to him. The dipper was cool, but the water still had the cattle smell of the creek. He wondered why they'd never sunk a seepage well, only he supposed that would require at least a small cash outlay, and an outfit like this wouldn't see fifty dollars a year.

"Thanks, ma'am," he said with careful courtesy. He looked from one of them to the other, and at the kids inside.

There were three, all boys, dressed in the sun-bleached, cast-off rags of their father. The oldest was about eleven. Somewhere he'd picked up a pair of boots that fit him. They were tallowed black, and some rough rawhide soles had been pegged on, but that didn't save the sides which were ruptured, letting his toes leak out.

"Hello, button," Pecos said, but the kid didn't answer him. He put his hat back on. He didn't know how to start. Then he laughed and said: "Well, you folks wouldn't believe me if I said there was four sides to a barn, but this is it . . . you and Ridley been making it pretty tough on each other. . . ."

"We make it tough on Ridley? Him and his big house, and his shiny carriage, and his fancy steppin' horses . . . ?"

"No-o, now hold on. He's spread out from here to yonder, I'll admit. But he won't have anything but the Medicine Ridge if you homesteaders keep fencing the water. You've fenced a whole site of it more'n you need, just like he grabbed more of the range than he needs. Upshot will be that each of you will keep pushing the other a little bit farther until all hell'll bust out. I came here on my own to advise you to try and get together . . . compromise a little."

"In what way?"

"Talk Harry Layne into taking down that reservoir dam he built that holds back the Little Sage. Make some cattle crossings on Horn Creek. Lot of those fences are built around nothing, just to push Ridley stock off the water. That's a dog-in-the-manger attitude, seh."

The woman cried: "You've got a lot of nerve talking to us about dogs in the manger when Ridley's forced the big steamboat outfits to refuse shipment even when they need our spuds and truck the worst way down at Benton and the minin' camps."

"Maude!" her husband said. "Let's listen to him."

"Excuse me, ma'am. I been trying to say it works both ways, and you both suffer. And maybe you'll suffer the most. Ridley's just started."

"If he tries to come down on *us* with his gunmen, he'll find. . . ."

"He'll not do that." Pecos pointed toward the Medicine Ridge. "You ride yonder . . . 'way yonder, where that long ridge with the jack timber on it runs out south from the peak. . . ."

"The Crow's Nest?"

"You go yonder. See what's doing. He's putting the old King Midas Mine into operation. Got a stampin' mill that'll grind rock like flour. When he's caught the gold, he'll run those tailings into the Big Sage. They ain't ordinary tails. They got a couple percent of lemon arsenic, besides sulphur, lime, and iron oxide. They'll yellow the bank, and kill the fish, and stink like sulphur smoke. Try to irrigate with it and your crops will shrivel up and die."

She said: "You can't scare us."

"I ain't trying to, ma'am. I got nothing to win. No matter who wins, I'll end up without a friend in the country. I got a pal hankering for Idaho, and I'm getting a hanker for it, too. It's just that I dealt myself a hand in a bad game, and now I don't know any way of getting out of it. I'm here tryin' my best to help you and Ridley both."

"He can't poison a stream. There's a law preventin' such a thing," Rutledge said.

"Sure. Down in black and white. In the territorial books, to be enforced by a bunch of millionaires in Helena, men that got rich out of Butte Hill and Last Chance. You think those big mining men would ever tell a gold mine to shut down because it contaminated a rancher's water supply? And even if the law did side with you, how long would it take?" Pecos kept talking in an easy voice. He hunkered, picked a wire-stiff spear of buffalo grass, and picked at his teeth with it. "You think it over. Talk it over with the others. I'll drop back in. . . ."

"You don't need to!" Rutledge got down and hitched up his gun belt. "I'll give you your answer right now. You go back and tell Ridley we don't scare. He can threaten what he wants to. We're here legal, and we're here to stay."

"Sorry." Pecos got up and limped back to his horse, still trying to kick the fatigue of riding from his legs. "I wish you'd think it over. I sure *do* wish you'd think it over."

XII

"Guns Aflame"

A week later, at The Citadel, four representatives of the Horn Creek Land Owners Association rode up—they were the Rutledge brothers, Gus Hyslop, and a spare, rooster-necked man named Cassman. Pecos walked to meet them. They were still by the gate, wary of trouble, although none of Ridley's eighty-a-month cowboys had so much as changed his sprawled position in the shade.

"You talked compromise," Harry Rutledge said. "Are you still talking it?"

"Seh, it's not up to me. Jawn Ridley's at the big house, though. You come yonder. No, you don't need to be wary. No matter what you think about Ridley, he's a Southern gentleman, and you're his guests. He'd kill any man that was even impolite while you're at his place."

Ridley had been watching from the front window, but he pretended to be taken by surprise. He had contempt for these hoemen, anger that Pecos had brought them to his house, but he hid both, ordered the Chinese servant to bring whisky, offered them cigars. Then he listened with a big-boned set to his jaw while Harry Rutledge told him what they'd come for.

He laughed bitterly and said: "You fence off my water, hog my range, and now you want to close down my mine!"

"We're here to compromise," Gus Hyslop said in his mild way.

"Then you have something to offer. What is it?"

211

"There's only a couple good homesteads on Horn Creek. We'll buy 'em out. Make room for 'em on the Sage. We'll stop damming the water and take down every fence that's not needed to protect our crops. We'll acknowledge the range is yours if you'll acknowledge the bottoms belong to us. What we've claimed, that is. We'll do that if you close the gold mill, and let us trade at the Landing." Then Hyslop dropped a bombshell. "We already sent a message to Judge Sturgis at Benton. Everybody knows he's fair and square. We'll abide by whatever he says. We asked him to come to Ridley Landing to arbitrate."

Ridley didn't speak for a few seconds, but Pecos knew how he felt by the savage way he bit into his cigar. He doubled his fists. His muscles thickened, tightening the shirt across his arms and shoulders.

Hyslop said: "You trust Judge Sturgis, don't you?"

"Yes, I trust Sturgis. He's the most respected man in the territory. A man who wouldn't trust Sturgis wouldn't trust anybody. If he'll come, I'll abide by anything he says."

Ten days later a special messenger arrived at Ridley Landing from the telegraph station at Fort Wells. Judge Sturgis was leaving for St. Louis on the steamboat *Dakota*, the last one downstream before low water ended river transportation for the season. However, as the *Dakota* would stop at the Landing to take aboard wood and freight, the judge would be willing to meet representatives of both factions in his stateroom. The date set by Sturgis was four days away, giving time to summon the farmers from Bull Creek and representatives of the 76 and the J Bar E far over by the Big Dry.

Wagons started rolling into Ridley Landing the afternoon before. About sundown, the Pecos Kid rode in with Al Ridley. He grinned at sight of the farmer wagons gathered in a circle around a cook fire.

"Like they expected a visit from Blackfeet!"

"Or from us Ridleys!" Al said, and he didn't smile.

"I notice you been worried about something."

"There'll be trouble."

"I doubt it. Judge Sturgis carries too much weight. Even for your dad. Nobody'd better start slingin' lead when Sturgis is around. He'd turn that steamboat around and go back for the Army."

They found every one of the Landing's keg and tincup saloons filled with 'punchers who'd ridden in with the representatives of the 76 and the J Bar E. More men kept arriving during the night, and the morning hours. The homesteaders stayed in their camp on the flats of the Big Muddy, while cattle outfits occupied the town. Only the little general store and one saloon at the lower end of town saw a mixture of both factions.

There was considerable drinking, but little noise. The men were holding their liquor. As the morning passed, a crowd accumulated down on the steamboat dock.

The river had dropped considerably during the past ten days. Off toward the middle some mudbanks had appeared just above the surface.

Old Gus Hyslop, half strangled by a hard collar, limped up in bulldog-toed shoes and said to Pecos: "That river looks mighty low. I'd hate to take so much as a rowboat down at this time of year."

"The *Dakota* draws only three feet of water. They'll get it down, all right."

Noon passed, and the hot hours of afternoon. The *Dakota* was many hours overdue. Only a few remained on the dock. There was a meeting among the homestead wagons, and speculation in the saloons. The rumor had gone around that the *Dakota* would not arrive—that Ridley had given orders to the steamboat company *not to let it arrive.*

Pecos had just stepped inside the Elkhorn Saloon when two gunshots, one close on the other, hammered the hot afternoon air. He turned and moved quickly back outside. Men were already running toward the general store. Someone was down in the shadow of the platform. There was a rig just beyond that had been loading supplies.

The shooting had frightened the horses, and they were trying to fight their way from the hitch rack. He recognized the team and buckboard. They belonged to Harry Rutledge.

A man on horseback swung briefly into view behind the store and was off at a gallop. Even from two hundred yards through the shifting heat glitter of afternoon, Pecos recognized him as Carris Garde.

He ran down the street. The quick-gathering crowd blocked him from the store platform. Big Jim Swing towered above the others. He was near the fallen man, trying to push the crowd back.

"Make room, damn it, make room!"

"Jim!"

Swing recognized Pecos's voice and looked.

"Jim, what happened?"

"That damned Carris Garde! He came up and caught Rutledge putting grub in the wagon. Started a row. Drew and shot him. This will let all hell loose." A tall, spare man with a goatee came up. Jim asked: "What is it. Doc?"

"He's dead. Died instantly." He got himself to the platform and looked over the crowd. "Has this man any relatives here?"

One of the Stinchfield riders back of Pecos said: "That's a hell of a note. He's got a wife and three kids."

It took a few minutes for the news to spread through the

homesteaders' camp. By that time Rutledge's body had been moved to the shed back of the store. The crowd broke away, and the town seemed quiet. Then, walking in a tight group, with rifles, shotguns, and six-shooters ready, the homesteaders came up the street.

The doctor, after some prodding, stepped out on the store platform and called: "What you aiming to do?"

Gus Hyslop took a couple of steps in front, spat tobacco juice, wiped his lips on the back of his hand, and said: "We want that killer . . . Carris Garde."

"The law'll take care of him."

He cried: "*We'll* take care of him, or we'll shoot this town apart."

Men of the ranch crowd stood under the awnings all along the street, listening. It was so quiet Gus Hyslop's words bounded in echoes from the cutbanks back of town.

Somebody said: "He already cleared out."

The Stinchfield cowboy back of Pecos said: "He did like hell. That yellow-gutted bushwhacker hid himself inside Long John's barn."

The barn he mentioned sat slightly back from the main street, on a knoll. The homesteaders started that way and were met by a volley of gunfire.

Shooting suddenly burst from a dozen other directions. One of the homesteaders went down, and two others dragged him to cover. On the instant, scarcely anyone was left in sight. Men were down behind sidewalks, between buildings. There was a hornets' nest of rifle fire behind some broken wagons and old iron heaped at the side of the blacksmith shop.

Caught from two sides, the homesteaders retreated. Pecos and Big Jim found themselves trapped with Hyslop, Fred Rutledge, and a couple other homesteaders against the west wall of the general store.

Bullets ripped in from a saloon across the street. Some gunmen from the Stinchfield Rranch had placed themselves there. Pecos crawled, came to a crouch. The leader of the Stinchfield gunmen showed himself in the door. They saw each other at the same instant. Pecos's bullet was a fraction of a time ahead, knocking the man down like he'd been hit by a sledge.

"That's one of the dirty killers," Hyslop said behind him. "Here, lemme up beside you with this scatter-gun."

Rutledge said: "They're outside . . . the back way." Through clenched teeth he was trying to fight back his emotions. "I'll get one of 'em. I'll get one for Harry!"

He fired and missed, and missed again. He had an old rimfire Henry, so shot out there was neither rifling nor accuracy left in the barrel.

The main group of homesteaders had now retreated to a ditch that made a natural fortification just below town. Bullets whipped back and forth, raising riffles of dust in the street. One of Ridley's eighty-a-month 'punchers was down, shot through the mouth, and two companions kept shouting through cupped hands for the doctor, but he was inside the door and refused to show himself.

Pecos and Jim had moved around to the rear of the store. It was there Hernandez found them.

"What, *señores?* You cower like two old squaws? What keeps you here? Is it the sound of lead bullets or the jingle of gold money you hope to be paid from the purse of that scoundrel, Jawn Ridley? I for one am seek of the whole business."

Pecos said: "Idaho's a fine place, Butch, but we got a few things to wind up first."

"Who talks of Idaho? Come, *señores!* I need a slight bit of help to march upon that stable and put bullets through the steenking insides of Carris Garde."

216

"No, Butch. You light for a while. You. . . ."

"Is thees the Pecos who outdrew Querno and Alderdice, both at the same time? Is thees the Pecos Keed I was proud to have for *amigo* because he said *to hell weeth danger* and rode in the teeth of feefty guns through the hot dust of Guadalupe? Has thees northern air chilled your blood? Have you been drinking the milk of the jack rabbit?"

"I sometimes take pride in shootin' one o' them Sam Colt things, but I also got a hanker to stay alive. Doing one and the other both at the same time requires a certain time and a certain place. That time and place ain't now. You bide a while, Butch. And don't think too hard about Carris Garde. We'll give him a day or two."

"*Señor*, weeth or weethout you, Hernandez Pedro Gonzales y Fuente Jesús María Flanagan will. . . ."

"Get down!"

XIII

"Time for a Showdown"

It had ended when evening settled. Pecos, Big Jim, and Hernandez rode along a buffalo trail through the back country hills. They covered a mile without speaking. Then Hernandez asked: "Where to, Keed?"

"I been thinkin' about it. Ridley ain't through yet. He won't let it stand half done."

"You theenk this judge, Sturgis, is also in the pants pocket of Ridley to be taken out and danced on a string whenever . . . ?"

"No. If that was the case, the judge would have got here. Ridley saw to it he *didn't,* and saw to it that all hell broke loose so nobody could ever get those homesteaders in to talk compromise again. But he still hasn't won. In some ways, Ridley's worse off now that he was before. He's a smart man, and a merciless man. He'll strike again and strike hard, before that G.A.R. bunch in Helena takes a hand."

"If we returned to The Citadel. . . ."

"We're through there. We'd better ride yonder to Rutledge's. I reckon he'd be alive tonight if it hadn't been for me."

Big Jim said: "You can't look at it that way, Kid!"

"I never been one to shirk my responsibility. And there's three ragged kids out there that's part of *my* responsibility."

Seven wagons were drawn up at the Rutledge place when

218

they arrived just before dawn. Gus Hyslop plodded out, still in his bulldog shoes, a shotgun in his hands.

"We'll go if you tell us to," Pecos said.

"No. I guess it weren't your fault. We talked it all over. Ain't a man here that thinks it was your doing. You come in if you'd like to. There's some coffee on the stove."

"I want to see Miz Rutledge. I got to tell her how I feel."

It was one of the hardest things he'd ever done. He came outside afterward, feeling sick and sweaty.

Hyslop said: "You look like you needed something stronger'n coffee." He pointed and squinted eastward. "Riders comin'. I guess we'll have a big funeral."

It was Cassman and the two Duckett boys from the Little Sage. They carried news of a rustler raid the evening before, and their places had been swept clean of stock—work horses, bronchos, milk cows, everything.

Tears glistened in Cassman's eyes as he talked. "That Daisy cow o' mine . . . you know what they did? Run her over a cutbank and broke her leg. Left her lyin' there. I had to shoot her. Best cow ever in the country."

Later, word came from Horn Creek that the raid extended even there. The Bull Sink gang had swept the country, timing it for the hours when everyone was camped at Ridley Landing.

They buried Harry Rutledge about noon. Afterward, the men held a powwow down near the creek that each day ran more yellow from the tailings of the King Midas Mine. They talked of riding against Bull Sink, against The Citadel, against the mine. Nothing was decided. Instead, they split into four groups to ride from farm to farm and gather additional men.

That was about two o'clock. Pecos agreed to stay on at Rutledge's until Harry Layne could drive back over with his wife and family.

"It's best not to leave the woman alone just yet," Layne, a short, pinkish gray, freckled man said. "You don't mind?"

Pecos said: "I'll do anything I can." After Layne drove off in his battered, rawhided wagon, he went in through the low doorway and looked at Maude Rutledge who, like a sleep-walker, was working around her kitchen. He turned his hat around in his hands and spoke. "Ma'am, you're left in a bad way with three kids."

"We'll make out." She sounded beat-out and tired.

"I got a little money. It's yonder." He tilted his head at The Citadel. It was more than a *little* money. It was the thousand in gold Ridley had given them. "I'll fetch it. It'll tide you over."

"I'm lookin' for no charity."

"You can owe it to me. I'll take a mortgage. That all right?"

"I suppose. I don't know . . . I suppose."

He went back outside. Mortgage! The whole place, chattels and all, wouldn't be worth four hundred. He'd get her name on the mortgage and tear it up.

He sat with Hernandez and Big Jim through the hot hours watching the yellowish creek flow past. The yellow had already crept up the bank, killing off grass and horse mint. Mrs. Rutledge prepared supper for them. Taste of the yellow was in everything—in the coffee, the food she cooked. Night settled, and there was a jingle of harness links as Layne drove back with his wife and kids.

"We'll go now," Pecos said.

"You leavin' the country?"

"Not for a while yet."

Mrs. Rutledge saw him leaving and ran from inside. She grabbed the latigo on his saddle and said: "I *will* give you a mortgage. How much do you think you could lend me?"

He looked far off, narrow-eyed, like a banker. They'd spent considerable money at the Landing, but Big Jim still had greenbacks sewed in his underwear from Miles City. "I'd say a thousand dollars, even. You sit tight. We'll bring it."

A mile from the ranch, Hernandez pulled his horse around and said: "Lone rider." He pointed with the glowing end of his cigarette. "In the willow brush, skirting it. I saw heem very plain. He seems to be following us."

"Stay here!" Pecos rode over alone. He kept his right hand upraised in the Indian signal of friendship, pulled up at long range, and called: "Hey, yonder!"

The answer was soft, but he could hear it across the night silence. "Keep coming!"

It was Letty Stinchfield. He should have been surprised, but he wasn't. He'd had a hunch.

She sat her horse very straight, both hands clutching the horn, waiting for him to come up. "You don't think any of *that* was my fault!"

It took him a moment to understand she was referring to the business at the Landing. "No, of course not."

"If I'd known . . . if I *had* known . . . !"

"Sure, Letty. You'd have told me. It was pretty rough. He had three kids."

She moved her horse over. He could feel her knee against his. She reached and had hold of his shirt a second before her horse turned and pulled them apart.

"Pecos! I lied to you once. I *did* tell Kansas you were a spy. I'm sorry now, after I saw how he played the game."

"You mean the raid last night?"

"Yes! I never cared for him. It was just. . . ."

She couldn't find the right words, and he said: "Sure, gal, I understand. It's all water over the falls. We got to start out

221

from *now*. You came to tell me something else, didn't you?"

"They're going to attack the mine?" She tilted her head, indicating the homesteaders over by the Big and Little Sage.

"I don't know."

"You still don't trust me?"

"Hold on. That's the truth. I *don't* know."

"Well, they *are*. Ridley had men trailing them, watching through field glasses. This evening they headed down the road toward Threesleep, and swung west at Ross Coulée toward the mine. Now he's getting ready to ambush them. I ran my horse all the way. I thought, if I couldn't find you, I'd head over and warn them myself."

"You think Ridley's already on his way?"

"Not yet. He had to bring some of his men up from the Landing."

"Al tell you all this?"

"Yes. He'd have come, only his dad has men watching. . . ."

He took hold of her arm. "You like the kid, don't you?"

"I don't know. You wouldn't understand. He needs me."

"Sure. That's a good thing about women. A good woman will go to the man that needs her."

He kissed her. "That's good bye," he said, and, driving his spurs, set off at a gallop.

"Pecos . . . !" she cried, but he didn't slow or look back.

He didn't stop for Hernandez and Big Jim. He motioned, and they galloped after him.

After a mile, Hernandez drew close enough to say: "What the hell? You wish to keel your horse, *señor?*"

Pecos shouted over his shoulder: "Those dumb Yankees have it in mind to attack the mine, and Ridley knows it. Maybe we get to The Citadel we can talk him out of layin' a deadfall."

"*Talk*, Keed? I have had enough of talk!"

Pecos slapped his gun and cried: "Enough of *this* kind of talk?"

"Ha, now you are the Pecos Keed of old. No, of that Colt music I have heard too leetle!"

The country steepened. They passed through scrub pine and juniper, down a shallow wash, around a rock point. There they could see the valley of Ridley Creek, with the home ranch and The Citadel below. By the cut-across route it had been a scant six miles from the Sage.

Pecos drew up and let his horse breathe. "Still there," he said, his voice showing relief. "See yonder? Heap o' men by that lighted-up house."

Hernandez cursed under his breath. "My guitar is in that bunkhouse. You do not theenk . . . ?"

"Don't worry about that damned guitar. Worry about the nine-fifty in gold coin I hid under my bunk."

They rode straight down to the corrals. Bronchos were galloping in a circle, and men were trying in the dark to get ropes on them. Over the running and shouting no one paid the slightest attention.

"Hadn't we better walk from here, Kid?" Big Jim asked, sounding short of breath from excitement.

"I'm enough of a cowboy to have contempt for walking. I aim to ride up yonder like a Southern gentleman."

They circled the corrals. A cowboy riding down from the bunkhouse peered at them through the dark—peered and kept peering but didn't speak. They dropped out of sight, splashed across the shallow creek, and emerged again.

Lamps and candles burned in the houses. The whole place was awake and busy.

Big Jim kept wiping sweat off his face. Hernandez, seeing him, laughed with music in his voice and said: "Save some of

223

your sweat. I theenk it will get much hotter."

Jim whispered: "You ain't figuring on riding straight up to the big house! There'll be men ten deep around there."

Pecos said: "Looks to me like they're ten deep all over."

There was an area of darkness between the ranch and the grounds of The Citadel. They climbed a steep pitch, followed the winding carriage path through shrubs and trees.

Jim, still wiping sweat off his vast face, whispered: "I didn't like the way that cowboy looked at us down by the corral. Rode by without speaking. Ain't natural. He suspected something."

"*Señor,* have I ever told you about the time in Chihuahua when I was in love weeth the daughter of a *bandido* chief who had keeled the last five men who tried . . . ?"

"No, and I don't want to hear it. Keep still, damn it! Hear that? There's somebody a-galloping."

"Listen, about thees woman, the *bandido's* daughter . . . starting from the ground she was like thees, and then she came out like thees, then like thees a man could put two hands around her waist, and then . . . ."

"Hold it, Butch," Pecos said. "They *are* galloping this way."

The hoofs made a sudden clatter in the dark behind and below. By the sound they split into two groups. They were still coming, but a little more slowly, circling the grounds.

A man called: "Carris!" It was Curly Wolfe, leader of those eighty-a-month gunhands.

Carris Garde answered from the region of the front porch. "What's wrong?"

"You got visitors coming up through the yard."

His voice sounded on edge. "What do you mean?"

"It's Pecos and his pals . . . that's what I mean."

Pecos said under his breath: "We get off here."

Jim whispered: "You *still* going on to the house?"

"I aim to pay Jawn Ridley a visit."

Pecos walked on, letting the bridle drag. Without looking around he knew that Hernandez and Big Jim were following. He fingered cartridges from the loops of his belt, and put them in his pocket where they'd be easier to get hold of. It was very quiet now. His boots crunched loudly on the gravel path.

He could see the front of the house, its porch, verandah, and big bay windows. He stopped. Somewhere a horse stumbled; a man cursed. Men were running around the house. He took another step; moonlight fell on him; a man jumped to the concealment of a porch pillar and fired. The bullet carried a sting of powder as it winged past his cheek. He shot back while going for cover.

Suddenly they were in a crossfire. They crawled through bushes, across a stretch of lawn to a rock garden of agate boulders where a fountain trickled, and Alpine plants were in bloom.

Hernandez had shot his six-gun dry. He lay in the cover of rocks, reloading. "Keed," he whispered. "Is thees Southern hospitality I have heard you speak so highly of? Keed, where are you?"

"I'm here, and you stay there."

He slid over the rocks. He was in the open for an instant. A slug dug the earth and beat one side of his face with stinging fragments.

Carris Garde shouted: "Curly. Get somebody by the east road in case they make a run for it."

Pecos smiled through his teeth. It hadn't occurred to them that they wouldn't try to escape. He kept moving through the bushes. He was only steps away from the porch.

A man grunted, lunged from the shadow, fell. He was wounded. Other men tried to pull him back.

Pecos, lying flat, used his elbows to drag himself across open ground. Shrubbery by the porch hid him. He was so close he could hear the wounded man grunt from pain. Gunsmoke and the stench of gunsmoke drifted over him.

The porch was above him. He got hold of some lattice-work, pulled himself over the rail. He rested on one knee, got his bearings. The big porch half circled the house. He moved along, past lighted windows, found a side door, opened it, and lightly stepped inside.

XIV

"A Job Well Done"

It was quite dark there. It seemed close and hot. The stale smell of cigars touched his nostrils. Gunfire sounded heavy, drum-like through the walls.

He walked down a short length of hall. A door led to the big sitting room. Light shone beneath it. As his hand touched the knob, the light went out. He opened the door, stepped inside. The large outlines of the room were revealed by a slit of lamplight coming from the front entrance hall.

"Carris?" It was Ridley. He was seven or eight steps away, in the middle of the room. He bellowed: "Carris!"

Carris Garde answered from out front: "Yeah, I'm here."

"Where are they now?"

"Still back of the rock pile."

"Smoke them out of there. If they're still alive, bring them in. I want a few words with that Pecos Kid." He laughed and added: "A few *last* words!"

Pecos walked on. He had a vague impression of Ridley's position. He didn't draw, but he was conscious of the weight of his gun. He said: "If you want to talk with me, Jawn, here I am."

His voice hit Ridley as though it had physical force. He spun. His breath came in a grunt of surprise. There was a shine of gunmetal, flame, and explosion.

Pecos had been on the move. The bullet whipped the air beside him. His own gun roared. The door to the front entry, that had been three or four inches ajar, now flew fully open. Silhouetted was Carris Garde with a gun in each hand.

He saw Pecos at the same instant. His guns blazed, but he'd shot too quickly. He'd made the mistake of not freezing his target. He tried to thumb the hammers and fire again, but his time had run out.

Pecos hit him with bullet lead. The three hundred grain slug knocked him backward. He hung with his back to the door casing and his legs thrust out stiffly. He fired into the floor. He tried to move, and his legs folded under him. His body struck the floor with a heavy, dead weight.

Pecos kept going. He exchanged shots with Ridley. Gunsmoke blinded him. His gun was empty. He grabbed cartridges and tried to reload. Suddenly Ridley loomed in front of him. He had time to thrust the man's gun up as it exploded. They reeled across the room, collided with the table.

He was no match for Ridley's strength. The man ripped free; with the same movement he flung him to the floor. Ridley covered him and pulled the trigger, but the hammer fell with an empty *click*.

He cursed and swung out with the barrel. He'd aimed at Pecos's head, but movement in the smoky half light made the blow miss. It struck with paralyzing force where the neck and shoulder joined.

Instead of following it up, Ridley started reloading his gun. Pecos's muscles were heavy; his veins seemed to flow molten lead. He managed to clinch, and keep the gun muzzle away from him. He held on desperately, getting the lead weight of paralysis out of his muscles, as Ridley dragged him across the room. A chair was underfoot. Ridley trampled it to disjointed rungs and kicked it away from him.

Strength was flowing back through Pecos's body. He had his sense of balance again. He was able to think and move. He knew by the tension of Ridley's muscles that he was preparing a massive effort to hurl him away. He let go of his own accord. It took Ridley by surprise. It made him take a step to regain his balance. Pecos, pivoting, brought up a right-hand blow with all the strength of his legs and back and arm behind it.

It caught Ridley at the apex of its power. It snapped his head as though he'd hit the end of a hangman's noose. The gun flew from his fingers. He reeled, hit the table, rebounded. Now it was Ridley who needed to grapple. Pecos took a step back, set his feet, and smashed him to the floor.

Ridley got up and ran headlong into a right and left. He staggered against the wall. He was staring and slack-jawed. The next blow dropped him on his back with his arms wide. Still he managed to roll over, drag himself to his knees. His eyes were out of focus. His mouth dropped open, and blood ran from the corners. His lips formed words. "No! Don't hit me again."

Pecos stepped back and got a deep breath. "All right, Ridley. Call your men. Tell 'em the ambush is off."

He nodded. He got to his feet, tripped, fell headlong, and got up again. He reached the window. He called to them, but the shooting still went on. He smashed the pane with his fist. Then he shouted: "Curly! Mike! That's enough. Get back . . . to the bunkhouse."

The shooting slowly came to a stop. He turned around. He took a couple of steps. The rug had been wrinkled. His toe caught, and he fell. One outstretched hand reached his fallen gun. He grabbed, twisted over, came to a crouch.

There were twin explosions—his gun and one outside the window, and the one from outside was a second ahead. It knocked Ridley forward and made his bullet fly wild. He lay face down, still working his arms, trying to get his gun, trying to rise.

Hernandez, walking across the porch, said: "*Señor* Keed, I did not keel heem. But I nicked him very good. Where is that back-shooter, Carris Garde?"

"There, on the floor."

"You have shot heem already? *Señor,* thees is a dirty way to treat me, the *amigo* of your heart!"

"Call to Jim! Get him in here before one of those gunhands takes a notion to shoot him in the back."

"Here I am, Kid!"

"Come here. Help me lift Ridley to the couch. Butch, you pull the shades and get the lamps lit. We'll have to get his bleeding stopped."

The bullet had struck a bone and glanced upward, missing the spine.

Pecos said: "You'll never come closer to killing a man than that, Butch."

"I never so wanted to keel a man without doing it. You know why I did not? Because his back was turned. But if he had been facing me. . . ." He shrugged and pointed to the wound. "That bullet I theenk shattered a vertebra. He will be months in bed with that. A year? Who knows?"

Later on they found Al Ridley locked in a room upstairs. Al said: "He found out I'd sent Letty away to warn you about the ambush. He was mad enough to kill me. Threatened to kill me. I guess I'm lucky."

"He won't be too tough to handle for a while," Pecos said.

"Will he live?"

"He'll live."

"I want him to live. I want him to live and be proud of me. I'll take care of him. I'll run the place. I'll square things with those homesteaders. Close the mill, pay the damage. And I'll settle the score with those rustlers at Bull Sink, too. You boys stay and help me. I don't know how much he offered to pay you, but I'll raise it."

"Sorry, Al. We got pretty important business elsewhere." Pecos laid a hand on his arm. "Some *very important* things to take care of in the Territory of Idaho."

At dawn they left The Citadel behind. To the south, rising straight and high against the morning horizon, was a pillar of smoke marking the position of the King Midas mill.

Hernandez, pointing it out, said: "There is one task taken care of already."

"Yeah. Those homesteaders meant business." Pecos kept tossing the bag of gold pieces from one hand to another. "We got to leave this yonder with Miz Rutledge. From there, I reckon, we'll head south through Threesleep to the N.P. How much money you got sewed in your drawers, Jim? Maybe we could load these bronchos in a stock car and ride 'em in style across the mountains to that silver town in Idaho. Always hankered to see Idaho. Butch, what was it about that place? Was it a six-story building filled to the roof with women?"

"Well, perhaps it is only *three* stories filled weeth women. What the hell? Cannot we make love to all of them twice?"